W9-CDO-453

MARVELLOUS STORIES from the Life of Muhammad

Mardijah Aldrich Tarantino

THE ISLAMIC FOUNDATION

Copyright © The Islamic Foundation 1982/1402H. Reprinted 1985, 1989, 1994, 2001 and 2008

ISBN 978 086037 103 8

All rights reserved. No part of this publication may be reproduced, stored in a retrieval system, or transmitted in any form or by any means, electronic, mechanical, photocopying, recording or otherwise, without the prior permission of the copyright owner

MUSLIM CHILDREN'S LIBRARY

MARVELLOUS STORIES FROM THE LIFE OF MUHAMMAD

Writer and researcher: **Mardijah A. Tarantino**

Illustrations: **Latifa Ahmad**

These stories about the Prophet and his Companions, though woven around authentic material, should still be read only as stories and should be treated as such.

Published by
The Islamic Foundation

Markfield Conference Centre,Ratby Lane,
Markfield, Leicester LE67 9SY, United Kingdom
Tel: (01530) 244944; Fax: (01530) 244946
Email: publications@islamic-foundation.com
Web site: http://www.islamic-foundation.com

Quran House, P.O.Box:30611, Nairobi, Kenya

PMB 3193, Kano, Nigeria

Distributed by: Kube Publishing

British Library Cataloguing in Publication Data

Tarantino, Mardijah Aldrich
    Marvellous stories from the life of
    Muhammad.-(Muslim children's library)
    1. Muhammad (Prophet) - Juvenile literature
    I.Title   II.Series
    297'.63   BP75

MUSLIM CHILDREN'S LIBRARY

An Introduction

Here is a new series of books, but with a difference, for children of all ages. Published by the Islamic Foundation, the Muslim Children's Library has been produced to provide young people with something they cannot perhaps find anywhere else.

Most of today's children's books aim only to entertain and inform or to teach some necessary skills, but not to develop the inner and moral resources. Entertainment and skills by themselves impart nothing of value to life unless a child is also helped to discover deeper meaning in himself and the world around him. Yet there is no place in them for God, who alone gives meaning to life and the universe, nor for the divine guidance brought by His prophets, following which can alone ensure an integrated development of the total personality.

Such books, in fact, rob young people of access to true knowledge. They give them no unchanging standards of right and wrong, nor any incentives to live by what is right and refrain from what is wrong. The result is that all too often the young enter adult life in a state of social alienation, bewilderment, unable to cope with the seemingly unlimited choices of the world around them. The situation is especially devastating for the Muslim child as he may grow up cut off from his culture and values.

The Muslim Children's Library aspires to remedy this deficiency by showing children the deeper meaning of life and the world around them; by pointing them along paths leading to an integrated development of all aspects of their personality; by helping to give them the capacity to cope with the complexities of their world, both personal and social; by opening vistas into a world extending far beyond this life; and, to a Muslim child especially, by providing a fresh and strong faith, a dynamic commitment, an indelible sense of identity, a throbbing yearning and an urge to struggle, all rooted in Islam.

The books aim to help a child anchor his development on the rock of divine guidance, and to understand himself and relate to himself and others in just and meaningful ways. They relate directly to his soul and intellect, to his emotions and imagination, to his motives and desires, to his anxieties and hopes — indeed, to every aspect of his fragile, but

3

potentially rich personality. At the same time it is recognised that for a book to hold a child's attention, he must enjoy reading it; it should therefore arouse his curiosity and entertain him as well. The style, the language, the illustrations and the production of the books are all geared to this goal. They provide moral education, but not through sermons or ethical abstractions.

Although these books are based entirely on Islamic teachings and the vast Muslim heritage, they should be of equal interest and value to all children, whatever their country or creed; for Islam is a universal religion, the natural path.

Adults, too, may find much use in them. In particular, Muslim parents and teachers will find that they provide what they have for so long been so badly needing. The books will include texts on the Quran, the Sunnah and other basic sources and teachings of Islam, as well as history, stories and anecdotes for supplementary reading. Each book will cater for a particular age group, classified into five: pre-school, 5-8 years, 8-11, 11-14 and 14-17.

We invite parents and teachers to use these books in homes and classrooms, at breakfast tables and bedside and encourage children to derive maximum benefit from them. At the same time their greatly valued observations and suggestions are highly welcome.

To the young reader we say: you hold in your hands books which may be entirely different from those you have been reading till now, but we sincerely hope you will enjoy them; try, through these books, to understand yourself, your life, your experiences and the universe around you. They will open before your eyes new paths and models in life that you will be curious to explore and find exciting and rewarding to follow. May God be with you forever.

And may He bless with His mercy and acceptance our humble contribution to the urgent and gigantic task of producing books for a new generation of people, a task which we have undertaken in all humility and hope.

Khurram Murad
Director General

Contents

Foreword and Preface   6

Introduction   7

 1 Abd Al-Muttalib and The Well of Zam-Zam   9

 2 The Feast of the One Hundred Camels   13

 3 The Spot   17

 4 The Caravan   19

 5 Bahira The Monk   23

 6 The Young Man   27

 7 The Call   31

 8 The Quraysh   37

 9 The Opposition   43

10 The Jinn   51

11 The Night Journey   57

12 The Cave   65

13 Madina   75

14 Madina II   81

15 The Battles: Badr   85

16 The Battles: Uhud   97

17 The Battles: The Ditch   105

18 The Return   111

Preface

This book is not only for Muslim children, but for all children, in the hope that it will awaken in them a feeling of who the Prophet Muhammad and his Companions were, and the times they lived in.

I ask God's forgiveness for any inaccuracies and pray that my good intentions will outweigh them.

Only God can know the truth.

Mardijah A. Tarantino

Foreword

A few words about this book.

I believe you will enjoy immensely reading these stories about our beloved Prophet Muhammad (may Allah's blessings and peace be upon him). At least for me it was a case of love at first sight. As soon as I had finished reading the manuscript, which arrived on my desk unsolicited, I decided to publish it. It is not very often that I receive such beautifully written manuscripts. I knew at once that Mardijah had an extraordinary talent for telling stories to children, stories which will hold their imagination for a long time to come.

To tell stories about our beloved Prophet is not so easy. No doubt his life is a limitless storehouse of priceless treasures which can be brought out and presented, for ever and ever, in an endless number of ways without ever exhausting their rich potentialities. Nevertheless his every word, his every deed, even his silence, is not only a source of light and joy for us but also an example to be followed. We Muslims are therefore very particular in recording and preserving his life, as accurately as we can. But we all know that children love to be told stories. Hence Mardijah chose to weave stories, for the children of today, out of the greatest ever human life story. We took some time to smooth out problems of historicity and editing. What has emerged may not be fully satisfactory to everyone, but there is no denying that she has been enormously successful in writing stories which will enchant many young hearts.

I now leave you to savour the charms and beauties that lie ahead.

Khurram Murad
Director General

Introduction

In the country of Arabia, about six hundred years after the life of Jesus, there lived a man called Muhammad, may Allah bless him. Muhammad had been a shepherd, and then a merchant. He could not even read or write, and yet he presented the world with a book — a book he had received from God — a book containing a new message and a new way of life for man; the laws of a new religion and the founding principles of a vast and powerful civilisation.

But now let us begin at the beginning: here is a story told by Muhammad's grandfather, Abd Al-Muttalib.

1

Abd Al-Muttalib and The Well of Zam-Zam

Late one night, long ago, an aged Arabic chief told this story to his little grandson, Muhammad. It all took place in Makka, an ancient city in the vast desert country of Arabia.

In Makka, there stands a sacred place called the Ka'ba. It has been sacred since the time of Abraham, perhaps even much earlier from the time of Adam. It was there, they say, that the Angel Gabriel presented the Prophet Abraham with a milk-white stone from Paradise. Since that time, the stone, according to the story, has been tarnished by the sins of man, and has turned black. So now it is called the Black Stone. Only a few pieces of it remain in the Ka'ba today, where Muslims from all over the world still come once a year on pilgrimage.

In the days of Abd al-Muttalib, Muhammad's grandfather, all kinds of other objects were heaped in the Ka'ba. There were strange oddly-shaped idols hewn out of red sandstone and other images carved into the shapes of men or godesses. There were magic statues called Hubal, Al-Lat, Al-'Uzza that were believed to have the power to make you rich, cure you of the plague, grant you a son, or bring you the princess of your dreams. Most of the pilgrims had forgotten about the One Almighty God, and had through the years become idolators, putting their faith and trust into a carved image made by man, rather than in the One God that created man in the first place.

They worshipped their odd-shaped images with

9

sacrifices, strange rites and chants; and in the evenings while squatting in front of the Ka'ba, they drank and gambled or threw arrows and darts trying to foretell the future, while the crowds of eager listeners would gather around the storytellers.

These storytellers, the poets of Arabia, could neither read nor write, but they had marvellous memories and would spin long tales in beautiful poetry all about the Jinns — the spirits of the desert as they described them, the Jinns who create mirages in order to trick the traveller into thinking there is cool water ahead... or who cause the sands to sing mysteriously at night, with a sound like distant laughter. The storytellers would tell tales of battles and lost loves, as well as give the latest news from far-away places. They had the power to twist the truth or ruin a man's whole life by a verse or clever piece of gossip. They were the newsmen of the desert.

Muhammad's grandfather Abd al-Muttalib was a chief and belonged to an important family called the Quraysh, descended from the Prophet Abraham. Aged and respected, he had his own place in the Ka'ba, in front of the Sacred Well. Beside him sat his little grandson Muhammad the orphan. Other members of the clan would waggle their beards in disapproval at the way Abd al-Muttalib spoiled his grandson.

'He is only six years old and instead of sending him off to bed, you allow him to stay up among adults into the dark hours of the night...'

Abd al-Muttalib felt it was no business of theirs; the boy had been left in his charge, after the death of his parents. So Muhammad, wrapped in his grandfather's great cloak, would listen half the night to the many stories old Abd al-Muttalib liked telling to the family and friends who gathered around. Usually Muhammad fell asleep when the words were too difficult to

10

understand, but tonight he knew that the stories his grandfather was telling were meant for his ears, too. And so he listened, his deep round eyes fixed on his grandfather's weathered skin and white beard.

'Now, when I was young and poor, and looked down upon by the wealthy members of my clan, my little son and I had the hard task of going from well to well, collecting water for the many pilgrims who came, as they still do, from far across the desert to worship at the Ka'ba. The wells around the Ka'ba were often empty or gave bad water. That was before the Sacred Well had been found. Now — before I go on — do you remember the story of this well — the sacred well of Zam-Zam?'

Muhammad smiled in response — he certainly did remember it. But Abd al-Muttalib continued anyway, because he loved to tell the story.

'Hagar and her little son Ishmael, the son of Abraham, were brought to live in the valley of Makka, where there was no water and nothing grew. Soon they were wandering hopelessly under the hot desert sun. But it was not God's will that they should perish. Lo! The Angel Gabriel appeared in a vision of light. He struck the sand and up gushed a crystal-clear spring of water right at the little boy's feet. That spring was named the well of Zam-Zam. But in the course of time the well disappeared, and no one even knew where it had once been. Well now, my little son had heard the story as often as you have, and one day he asked me, "Father, would a spring of water brought forth by the Angel Gabriel dry up and disappear forever?"

'I answered that if it was a sacred well, it certainly should not dry up. Then he asked me, "If that were so, then, Father, where is it now?"

'Ah! That is what started us looking. We began digging and we dug for days and weeks. The winds kept

11

shifting and the heavy sands filled in the holes we were digging again and again. Still we kept on and on, even though people — and members of my own clan — shrugged their shoulders in disgust or called out mockingly, "You are looking for a needle in a sandstorm!" But you see, I was convinced. I was so sure we would find the well that I made a promise to myself and to God:

'If the sacred well of Zam-Zam is found, there will be no more laughter, there will be praise: and my name will be spoken with respect by the people of Makka and by my clan the Quraysh. Therefore, if I am blessed with ten sons, the tenth shall I offer up to the Almighty God.

'And then a remarkable thing happened. My spade struck something hard, and I unearthed two huge pieces of gold in the shape of gazelles. Right underneath where they had lain the sand was dark and moist — and the waters of Zam-Zam rose before our very eyes and filled the hole where the gazelles had been. Of course, some people were more interested in the gold than in the well, but I told them that the gold belonged to the Ka'ba, and if you look when you leave, you will see, Muhammad, the two gold disks hanging over the entry of the Ka'ba. From that day on the sweet waters of Zam-Zam have gushed forth generously for the pilgrims. And you see that your grandfather is praised and respected!'

At this the others smiled and nodded.

'And I was given a title: Keeper of the well of Zam-Zam, and my place is not out there, under the hot sun, but here in the shade of the Ka'ba, by the Sacred Well.'

Muhammad, instead of going to sleep, was more awake than ever. His grandfather, seeing this, continued with another story.

2
The Feast of the
One Hundred Camels

'And now, I shall tell you about the Feast of the One Hundred Camels. What a noble beast the camel is! How valuable to the Arab people, think of it! What animal can go for twenty-five days without water? Why, a man under such circumstances would have perished long before the twentieth!

'Now tell me, my little man who once lived with the Bedouin, how did they cook their meals and heat their bodies on cold desert nights?'

Before Muhammad had a chance to answer this question and the others that followed, his grandfather had answered them himself and gone on with the story.

'Why, they used camel's dung for fuel and heat', continued his grandfather. 'And what did someone discover long ago, when his skin bag full of camel's milk had been shaken up on a long trek across the desert? Why, cheese, of course! And what is the tastiest meat of all, after a long day's journey? The meat of a camel, well roasted until tender. And what, tell me, is used to make the best tents? A camel hide. And this is his last offering to man. Without the camel, no one would be able to survive in this country of deserts. So that is why, you see, my little one, a camel's life according to tradition, may be worth the life of a man'.

Abd al-Muttalib turned to the elders then, and proceeded with his story in a deep but quiet voice.

'After this boy's father was born, I was faced with an awful reminder. I had made a pledge to God, and the time had come for it to be fulfilled. Perhaps some of

13

you remember that night? Indeed, how could anyone forget who had been present at the time.

'The air was so still as to be stifling. The shadows sharp and unrelenting before the sacrificial altar where my sons and I had gathered. Surely, they must have foreseen a sombre event, yet they did not hold back. I told them about the pledge — that when I was still young and searching fervently for the well of Zam-Zam, I made a promise to God, if he should give me 10 sons to grow to maturity to help me with my work, that I would sacrifice one of them near the Ka'ba... how proud a father I was in the secret of my heart, when they all consented. Then, you remember, the arrows of chance were drawn, and his name... my beloved 'Abdullah's name... was called out.

'Ah, my heart turned to ice within my breast. Yet, girding up my courage and will I clasped my young son by the hand and led him, with determined steps, to the sacrificial altar. It was at that instant... do you remember?... that cries of compassion arose and a voice proclaimed "Hold! Father of 'Abdullah, stay your hand! This cannot be!"

'I turned, stunned and confused to face the assembly. The men of the Quraysh were gathered in fervent consultation.

'"We have decided", they announced, "to consult the sorceress of Madina... and we are off to see her now!"

'Well, two long days went by before the answer came. And again we gathered between the sacrificial idols, while the decision of the sorceress was announced:

"One arrow shall be for ten camels, the other arrow with the name of your son. Ten camels shall equal the life of your son. If the arrow drawn is that of your son, then multiply the number of camels, and

14

draw again... keep drawing until God is satisfied."

'Again and again we threw the arrows until finally the camel's arrow was drawn, and the number of camels to be sacrificed was 100. With tears on my cheeks and thanks in my heart I embraced my young son.

'What great rejoicing there was in the city that night! One hundred camels were sacrificed, and we prepared a huge feast. All the citizens of Makka, down to the very poorest, were given a generous share: it was said that even the little beasts of the desert partook of the scraps. And until this day, no one — and I'm sure none of you were present — has ever forgotten the Feast of the One Hundred Camels.'

The lights of the Ka'ba were growing dim. Abd al-Muttalib gathered up his grandson in his huge, warm cloak, while the others took leave of him and made their way home through the dark, and narrow winding streets.

Those who had just listened to the tale did not dream — nor did anyone else in Makka at that time — that 'Abdullah of the One Hundred Camels had indeed served God's purpose; not as a sacrifice but as the father of Muhammad, God's Messenger, later to be called the Last of the Prophets.

3
The Spot

The Merchants of Makka were a clever lot. They bargained and sold their striped cloth from Yemen and their sweet smelling oils and perfumes at an ample profit to the pilgrims and travellers who bustled through their dusty crowded streets. They traded in dates, raisins and hides with which they stocked their camel caravans bound for other lands. They were clever, but not strong and healthy, and they spoke a colourless Arabic.

For this reason, some of the mothers of the chief tribes, like the Quraysh, sent their children to the desert to be raised by the Bedouin.

Beyond the city and far out into the desert lived these nomadic Bedouin Arabs. Unlike the Makkans they spoke a pure Arabic, but they were harsh and fierce. They had to be fierce and courageous to survive the ordeals of the desert: the sandstorms and the scorching sun, the cold dark lonely nights under the stars. They were called the Pirates of the Desert because they plundered other tribes in sport, and moved from oasis to oasis with their tents and cattle, seeking pasture. They were proud and had a high sense of honour and were loyal to their tribes. Above all, they were hospitable. They knew that no one, not even an enemy, should be turned out into the desert to perish.

Now before Muhammad had come to live with his grandfather, his mother Amina had placed him with the Bedouin Arabs so that he too would grow strong and healthy and speak a pure Arabic.

One day the time came for him to return. Mounted on a camel the boy and his Bedouin nurse Halima made their way back to Makka. They reached Amina's house and were welcomed and given food. Then the two women began to speak in whispers while the child stayed at a distance. The nurse was telling a strange story about the child she had brought back home.

'He told me that when he was tending the sheep two strangers — dressed all in white like angels — appeared out of nowhere. They laid him on the ground and opened his chest and removed a black spot from his heart... then they closed his chest again — and disappeared!'

Amina spoke with hesitation. 'Perhaps... perhaps. It is but the story of a child?'

'Yes, but you see', insisted the nurse, 'I saw the two strangers with my own eyes. I saw them come from out of nowhere and I saw them disappear'.

Amina bowed her head and was silent. And what she thought of this story we will never know, for she didn't live long enough after that to tell about it.

4
The Caravan

And so, Muhammad, the little orphan who had lost both his father 'Abdullah and his mother Amina, was placed in the care of his grandfather, the Keeper of the well of Zam-Zam. Those days were happy ones, because the old man and the boy truly loved one another. But finally, old Abd al-Muttalib's time came to leave the earth, and with his death, the days of Muhammad's childhood came to an end.

He was led to the home of his uncle, Abu Talib, feeling sad and very lonely. Abu Talib did his best to make a home for the boy, and he must have succeeded, because before long Muhammad began to console himself. But never in all the days of his life would he forget that he had once been an orphan without a mother or father to care for him.

His new life was entirely different from anything he had known before. Uncle Talib was neither a storyteller nor a dreamer. He was a not very successful Makkan merchant, and had no time for tales of angels or by-gone prophets. He spent his days and nights worrying about the stock of his merchandise and calculating the results of his business ventures.

Muhammad was twelve years old when his uncle began preparing for a long trade trip. His own camel caravan was going to make the long journey to Syria. The camels had to be examined, the packs secured, the merchandise accounted for, the supplies of water checked, and now, finally, the caravan was ready for departure. The night before the caravan was to depart,

Muhammad could not sleep. More than anything he wanted to accompany his uncle on the trip to Syria.

The next day Abu Talib was shouting orders and checking and re-checking the merchandise, while Muhammad stood by and watched. Finally, not able to hold himself back any longer, he rushed up to his uncle, grabbed his hand and pleaded that he be allowed to accompany him. Abu Talib was taken aback. Muhammad had never acted this way before, but the intensity in the dark eyes of his nephew could not be ignored. 'Well if you must', he said, 'you may join us'.

More orders were shouted, and the long caravan began its trek across the sands, winding its way through towns and oases, and back into the desert again. There was plenty of time for the telling of tales and plenty of opportunity for Muhammad to listen, his great dark eyes shining, to what was being told; and late at night, under the stars of the desert he lay wondering about the meaning of the tales he had heard.

He wondered about the Thamud, the giant people who had hewn their homes out of solid rock — the same rock the caravan had passed at sundown that day. God had created a mighty camel out of that rock, as a sign of His great power, and had entrusted it to the Thamud who were to care for it and allow it to graze wherever it wished on God's land. But in their resentment and usual disregard for the will of God, they had hamstrung the beast, whose wails could be heard throughout the heavens, and by this act, had brought about their punishment and the total destruction of their race.

Muhammad pondered on this. And what of the other story he had heard that day — of a certain tribe of the faith of Moses that had disregarded the laws of their religion and shunned the hours of prayer, and in their

greed for wealth, worked and sweated through every Sabbath day? It was said that for their pains the angels had turned them into monkeys — the only creatures of God having neither dignity nor code of law.

As he was falling off to sleep, Muhammad wondered about all these things. And he thought about his own city of Makka. He remembered the loud laughs of the drinking men, the look of the women he had seen in the streets, the gamblers with their cries of disappointment, the grotesque forms inside the Ka'ba; and he thought of his uncle, working late into the night, huddled over his accounts, and suddenly he was afraid for them all.

5
Bahira The Monk

Muhammad had never in his life heard such joyful sounds! From all directions came the ringing and tolling of bells as Abu Talib's caravan approached the Syrian town of Busra the following noon.

'Are they welcoming us?' Muhammad asked his uncle.

'Those are Christian church bells, calling people to prayer', explained Abu Talib. Muhammad kept silent when he heard that. It was an idea which interested him, but he knew little about it.

After the monotonous days of travel in the desert, this clean little town was a welcome sight to the travellers. It had rained recently, leaving patches of green here and there. The air was filled with an odour of damp earth and wet clay bricks. Suddenly the bells stopped ringing and everything became still. Muhammad breathed in the cool, moist air and felt refreshed. What a different place, he thought, from our hot, dusty, noisy Makka!

While Muhammad was thinking these thoughts, something quite unusual was taking place not far from him, in the cell of a Christian monk.

The monk's name was Bahira. He wore a long, unbleached tunic, had a shaven head and a long beard. He was a goodly soul and led a simple pious life in his cell on the outskirts of Busra.

Now on this particular day, while Bahira was tending to his devotions, he could hear, not far off, the sounds of an approaching caravan. This was a

23

commonplace thing, since year after year the caravans passed his way. What was unusual, what astounded him, in fact, was that this time he could actually see the caravan approaching before his closed eyes! There were the camels and the provisions, there were the men, bent over and tired from their long journey under the scorching sun, and there was a young boy — such a handsome young boy! — thought Bahira — riding in the midst of them. And what was more remarkable, the boy seemed to be accompanied by a cloud... his own personal cloud sheltering him from the sun! Bahira blinked and tried to look closer, but the image vanished and there remained only the bare, white walls of the cell.

Bahira got up from his knees as quickly as he was able and went to see this for himself. Under a nearby tree he saw the exact same caravan, and as he watched, the tree... a plain, simple tree, bent itself over until its leaves and branches overshadowed the figure of the handsome little boy — the same boy he had seen while praying in his cell!

Now, Bahira knew well that such things do not happen every day nor to ordinary people. 'Certainly this is a sign from God' he said to himself. 'This boy must bring with him a very special blessing...' At which point, an idea occurred to him, and he approached the caravan.

'Oh men of Quraysh, I have prepared food for you, and I should like you all to come, both great and small, bond and free.'

One of them laughed and answered, 'By God, Bahira, what extraordinary thing has happened to you today? You have never treated us in this way before, and we have often passed by you'.

Bahira was a little embarrassed by the truth of this observation. 'Ah, ahem! You are right in what you say

— but I wish you to be my guests. I wish to honour you with a humble feast.'

While Bahira carried out the preparations, Abu Talib turned to Muhammad. 'Here is your portion of food, Muhammad, be the good boy that I know you are, and guard our camels and provisions until we return.'

Muhammad didn't mind this at all. He was quite happy to sit alone for a change, and under the shade of the tree, to eat his meal quietly and think his own thoughts.

But Bahira was not happy in the least. Everyone was seated for the feast, but where was the boy? After all, it was really for him that he had prepared all this, but there was no sign of him. Could he have imagined it all, the boy, the cloud, the tree? Surely not! He was not yet an old fool! His hands shaking with impatience he repeated 'Do not let one of you — not one remain behind and not come to my feast'.

'By Al Lat and Al 'Uzza, we are to blame for leaving behind the young Muhammad' remembered one of the men, who then went to fetch him, embraced him and brought him to the feast.

All through the meal Bahira could not tear his eyes away from the young lad. How noble looking he was, in spite of his youth, how polite and humble, yet frank and steadfast in his gaze.

As soon as the feast was over, Bahira called him to his side. 'Sit here, beside me, boy, and tell me, by Al Lat and Al 'Uzza, all about yourself.' Bahira hoped he had got the names of those gods correct, so as not to offend the boy.

Now the story goes, at this point, that Muhammad corrected him and said 'Do not ask me by Al Lat and Al 'Uzza, for by Allah, nothing is more hateful to me than these two'.

25

So Bahira hastily put the question another way. 'Then by Allah, tell me what I ask' and then he began to ask Muhammad all about himself, and in all the answers that Muhammad gave, there was something which pleased the old man and made him feel certain that this boy was indeed someone blessed by God.

At last, Bahira led the boy back to his uncle. 'Guard him carefully', he cautioned Abu Talib, 'a great future lies before this nephew of yours'.

When Abu Talib came to fetch Muhammad, the monk and the boy were deep in conversation. On that day, Muhammad no longer felt alone in the world. He had found a friend.

'Do you think', asked Muhammad of his uncle on their way back to Makka, 'do you think that some day I might be allowed to return with you to Syria, Uncle?'

'Perhaps, why?'

'I was happy there', answered Muhammad.

'The next time you return to Syria', said his uncle, looking laughingly in his direction, 'it will be to help in the work of buying and selling! Not just to sit around wasting time in idle talk!'

Muhammad bowed his head and smiled.

6
The Young Man

'Look, Muhammad is back! There's Muhammad!'

A medley of ragged children raced with each other down one of the narrow Makkan streets to meet the young man who was just leaving the bazaar. They vied with each other to hold his hand; they chanted rhymes and skipped alongside him through the crowded streets.

Hearing the commotion, one little girl with silver bracelets stopped playing at the steps of her house, seized her little brother by the arm and ran with him in the direction of the children.

'Where are we going? Who's Muhammad?' he asked, dragging his toy bow behind him in the dust.

'Why, you know, he's the one who always feeds a carrot to Aswad's donkey as he goes by, and stops to pet our cat.'

'Will he feed me a date?'

'Yes, but hurry, or we'll miss him.'

'Are you going to meet Muhammad?' called out an older girl who tried to catch up with them in spite of her ankle-length dress. 'He's such a handsome man', she went on, 'and do you know, he must be the most well-groomed man in Makka: his hair and beard are always clipped and never ragged looking like Abu Afak's, and his teeth are always clean and shiny...'

'That's because he uses a toothpick when he thinks people aren't looking' confided the younger girl with delight, 'and he smells sweet because he hates onions and never eats them!'

'It's the oils and perfumes he uses, silly' answered the older girl as they caught up with the others.

Two older boys turned around to look, and seeing Muhammad in his white robe, went to join the others.

'So he's back', said one with a stubble of a beard. 'I've missed seeing him around. He's never too busy to say hello to us. He doesn't walk around with long scowls like some people — you know who I mean —' he said, nudging the other and looking in the direction of a group of elderly rich merchants on their way to the bazaar.

'Come on', he said with an air of importance, 'I'm going to ask him about the journey'.

Muhammad tried to answer all their questions while distributing, as fairly as he could, among the younger ones, the dates he carried with him for such occasions. Muhammad, in his early twenties, had become a successful merchant; not so much because he liked his work, but because he was honest in his dealings and could be trusted. He never overpriced his goods, nor skimped on weights, and usually gave other merchants the benefit of the doubt. Because of this, they called him 'Al-Amin' which means 'The Trustworthy', and this became his nickname.

On that morning, Muhammad was on his way to meet someone. His uncle had sent him to see the wealthy widow Khadija who was requesting an overseer for her caravans. Abu Talib had said that morning: 'Now Muhammad I would love you to stay with me but, as you know, my business is not going too well. Khadija needs someone to look after her trade and has asked if I could spare you.' So Muhammad presented himself to the widow.

Khadija looked up from her account books and was pleased with what she saw. The handsome young man in front of her with his high dark eyes and neat appearance impressed her.

'I am looking for an honest man who will take charge of my caravans on their various journeys. Abu Talib, your uncle, has recommended you to me. Would you be interested in such a position?'

Muhammad, who was never hasty, remained silent for a while and then accepted the job. Together they sat and discussed the responsibilities he would undertake: the number of beasts required for each caravan, the quantities of food and water to be stored, the kinds of merchandise and the prices they might fetch; and finally, the routes most favourable and the time of year of the departures. When all this had been gone over, Muhammad took leave of his new employer, and as he turned to go, Khadija called after him:

'I hear they call you "Al-Amin", "The Trustworthy".' Her kind face broke into a smile. 'I hope that while you are in my employment you will live up to your name!'

Muhammad blushed slightly and assured her that he would.

Muhammad did indeed live up to his name. He worked very hard, as Khadija had given him the management of all her caravans. His time was spent travelling across deserts and through oases to distant lands and foreign cities — to Damascus, to Jerusalem, and Aleppo. Khadija, each time he left, waited more and more eagerly for his return.

One day a surprising thing happened. Khadija's personal maid came to see Muhammad privately. She came with a marriage proposal from Khadija! Muhammad was astounded. He had never even had a girl-friend. He had never thought much about women, nor had he ever been close to one since the death of his mother. Some time back, when he was tending sheep, some shepherds passing by had called to him:

'Come to town with us tonight, Muhammad — we'll have a little fun with the girls!'

Muhammad, who liked the idea well enough, agreed to join them later. But he never turned up at the rendezvous. The following day the shepherds asked him:

'What happened to you last night?'

'Well', Muhammad confessed, 'when the time came, I fell asleep'. Of course they all burst out laughing and he joined in with them.

But Khadija, in the eyes of Muhammad, was a very special lady. She was warm and kind, and still quite beautiful despite the fact that she was older than he. This time, Muhammad did not take long to accept. The marriage between Muhammad and Khadija took place, and turned out to be a very happy one.

7
The Call

The two Makkan merchants watched as the dust from Muhammad's caravan cleared, and until they could see the heavily laden camels making their way slowly towards Yemen. The older of the two was Abu Lahab, another of Muhammad's uncles. Under his grey beard the corners of his lips turned down as he remarked: 'So! The young Quraysh orphan has made good. Not so stupid after all, even though he can't read. Clever enough to have won Makka's most sought-after widow, thereby gaining wealth and position all in one throw. An admirable scheme!'

'I'm not so sure', replied the other, 'that it was through scheming he arrived at all this. Fortune has indeed smiled upon him, despite the death of al-Qasim his son, which leaves him only four daughters. His wife is still beautiful and most capable. It is because of her that he has gained command of Makka's best equipped caravans. Yes, indeed, he is most fortunate... I would that my son had done as well...'

But no one, save Khadija perhaps, could have known what Muhammad was feeling at that very moment. He was in fact ashamed that he could not be more grateful for all that fate had given him. He could not feel grateful because he felt suffocated and imprisoned in his work. The buying and selling of worldly objects left him bored and dissatisfied. He knew for a certainty that his role on this earth was not that of a merchant. He found a merchant's life a narrow and empty one. His soul yearned for expansion and

بِسْمِ اللَّهِ الرَّحْمَنِ الرَّحِيمِ

حم ۞ وَالْكِتَابِ الْمُبِينِ ۞ إِنَّا أَنْزَلْنَاهُ فِي لَيْلَةٍ مُبَارَكَةٍ إِنَّا كُنَّا مُنْذِرِينَ ۞ فِيهَا يُفْرَقُ كُلُّ أَمْرٍ حَكِيمٍ ۞ أَمْرًا مِنْ عِنْدِنَا إِنَّا كُنَّا مُرْسِلِينَ ۞ رَحْمَةً مِنْ رَبِّكَ إِنَّهُ هُوَ السَّمِيعُ الْعَلِيمُ ۞ رَبِّ السَّمَوَاتِ وَالْأَرْضِ وَمَا بَيْنَهُمَا إِنْ كُنْتُمْ مُوقِنِينَ

In the name of God, Most Gracious, Most Merciful.

1. Hā-Mīm.

2. By the Book that
   Makes things clear;—

3. We sent it down
   During a blessed night:
   For We (ever) wish
   To warn (against Evil).

4. In that (night) is made
   Distinct every affair
   Of wisdom,

5. By command, from Our
   Presence. For We (ever)
   Send (revelations),

6. As a Mercy
   From thy Lord:
   For He hears and knows
   (All things);

7. The Lord of the heavens
   And the earth and all
   Between them, if ye (but)
   Have an assured faith.

   (Sūra 44 Al-Dukhān 1-7)

contemplation of the mysteries of life and death, and of man's responsibilities towards God and towards himself. He realised that such answers could not be found in the Ka'ba, as it was then filled with idolatry and superstitions, nor in his work, nor at home. There was only one thing left for him to do — to search within himself, and at these times words in the form of a prayer would burst forth from his lips: 'May I be led out of the darkness — may I be shown the true way...'

When he returned from a journey he would beg leave of his wife and would, for a time, turn to the life of a shepherd and seek freedom under the huge expanse of starlit skies that he had known as a child. There he could be close to the simple gentle nature of sheep, the quiet water of the oasis and the majesty of the night. Only then did his feelings become wide and calm. Often he fasted, and Khadija would ask him, perplexed, 'What, Abu al-Qasim (Father of al-Qasim) what! You are fasting on a work day? Why do you make things more difficult for yourself?'

And Muhammad would reply, 'It is easier, really, when I fast — then my work becomes more like a game than work, and I feel less heavy and bored'.

At other times to free his head of weights and measures, he would walk away from Makka to the hills of Hira. He came to spend more and more of his time there, fasting and praying, pondering and reflecting, trying to find answers to the questions which riddled his soul. During these long absences, Khadija would send him food which would last quite a few days.

It was on an odd night during the last ten days of the month the Arabs called Ramadan that Muhammad, once again, climbed the mountains of Hira and spent a day of fasting and a night of prayer sitting in his usual place.

Much later, when the night was at it's darkest, just

34

before the break of dawn, he heard a voice. This voice grew louder and louder and seemed to come from all directions, from around the cave, from beyond in the night, and from within Muhammad himself. He looked around and there appeared to him an angel who was holding a coverlet of green brocade upon which some writing was embroidered.

'Read!' commanded the being.

Muhammad was stunned. 'What shall I read?'

The angel squeezed him hard in embrace, and then released him.

'Read!' the angel commanded once more.

'What shall I read?' exclaimed Muhammad, a little louder this time.

Again the angel embraced him — and the embrace was tighter than before.

'Read!' commanded the angel for the third time.

'What shall I read!', replied again Muhammad who was fearful of another embrace.

'Read!' continued the angel, 'IN THE NAME OF THY LORD WHO CREATED MAN FROM A DROP OF BLOOD: READ IN THE NAME OF ALMIGHTY GOD WHO TAUGHT MAN THE USE OF THE PEN AND TAUGHT HIM WHAT HE KNEW NOT BEFORE...'

Muhammad repeated these verses after the angel, word for word, until he could recite them perfectly.

Soon he was alone. The angel and the writing had gone. Only the words remained, carved forever upon his memory. And there was also an extraordinary sensation in his body... of having been held in a very tight embrace.

Suddenly Muhammad was fully conscious and stricken with panic. 'Woe is me' he exclaimed to himself. 'Is the cave haunted? Am I a man possessed?' He arose, trembling with awe and began to wander out of the cave and down the mountain path, when a

35

voice... the very same voice... called to him from the heavens:

'OH MUHAMMAD! TRULY THOU ART THE
MESSENGER OF GOD
AND I AM HIS ANGEL, GABRIEL'

Muhammad looked up and beheld the angel in a human form — so enormous that his two feet straddled the horizon. Muhammad gazed up at him for a moment, and then turned to escape. But no matter in which direction he looked the angel was there, filling the entire sky. Helpless, Muhammad just stood, neither advancing nor turning back, until Gabriel disappeared from the skies as suddenly as he had appeared. Only then did Muhammad, in the light of dawn, slowly make his way down the path, through the hills to his home.

8
The Quraysh

When Muhammad — whom we shall now call the Prophet or God's Messenger — reached home, he confided to his wife everything that had happened. He told her about the sudden appearance of an angel whose bright form filled the skies from the horizon to the zenith. He recited to her the marvellous verses which he had been told to learn, and Khadija clasped her hands and exclaimed, 'Praise God', for she had no doubt that Muhammad had been chosen to be God's Messenger.

But a while later, he turned to her again, troubled. Taking her hand in his he looked into her eyes as if to find the answer to his question.

'Perhaps I have been approached by the very spirits and jinn which come to soothsayers and fortune tellers? Perhaps a cunning devil has come to trick me?'

Khadija drew her husband close to her and gently stroked his head. 'My dear Abu'l-Qasim, that would not be possible. For never since I have known you have you acted in a manner not worthy of praise. Are you not called "The Trustworthy"? Is not everyone a witness to your fine character? For you to be influenced by a spirit or a devil would be impossible. And what is more' — she added — 'I have been to see my old cousin Waraqa, who knows all there is to know about the religion of the One God; and when I described to him what had happened to you, his old face lit up, "Why, that is the Angel of Revelation!" he said. "It is he who brings the Good Word to the prophets of God. It is he who came to Abraham and to Moses".'

Upon hearing this, the Prophet raised his head and seemed to be calmed. He trusted and respected Waraqa, and knew him to be a wise man.

Months passed, as if nothing had ever happened. The Angel Gabriel did not appear again. There was no further revelation. The Prophet Muhammad became silent and distant while Khadija watched over him, waited with him, and consoled him as best she could.

Then one night, as unexpectedly as on the first night, the Angel once again appeared. With his finger outstretched as if to point the way, he awoke the sleeping Prophet with these words:

'O thou wrapped in a mantle!
Arise! And deliver thy warning!
And magnify the Lord!'

From that time on, the Angel appeared often. The Prophet received from him many revelations in beautiful Arabic which he was told to recite aloud, and which he then did recite to his followers. They in turn learned them by heart, and wrote them down. Much later, they were compiled into a book which is called *The Glorious Koran*. And who were these followers? At first, only his wife Khadija, his dearest friend Abu Bakr and two boys, whom he had adopted after the death of his sons. One was Zayd, a former slave boy from Abyssinia, and the other was his cousin 'Ali, a younger son of Abu Talib, his uncle.

'Ali was not much to look at, with his skinny legs and small stature, but he adored the Prophet Muhammad, and was to prove this many times during his life.

Muhammad's best friend was Abu Bakr. Abu Bakr trusted Muhammad more than he did any man in Makka and he knew that anything Muhammad had said had to be the truth. Besides Khadija, 'Ali and Zayd, he was the first man to hear of Muhammad's vision, and the first to declare without hesitation his belief in the One Almighty God.

Abu Bakr, who was a trader, was a very popular man in Makka. People who respected and loved him were always coming to discuss their problems or to ask him questions. Little by little he began to tell them about the new religion, Islam, and one by one they came to Muhammad to hear the marvellous messages he was receiving from Gabriel. Then they would quietly join the little band of believers to the outskirts of Makka where they held their prayers.

Three years went by, and then one day Gabriel appeared to Muhammad with a new command:

'Warn, O Muhammad, your nearest relatives...
And lower thy wing to the Believers who follow thee.'

The time had come for Muhammad to bring his message to the other important members of the family of Quraysh. But how would they ever accept what he had to tell them? How would they ever willingly give up their gods and goddesses for the worship of only One God? He felt sure the whole thing would lead to trouble, yet this was God's command, and Gabriel had told him that if he did not obey, he would be punished. The only thing left to do was to put everything in God's hands. Having made this decision, he turned to his beloved cousin, who was like a son to him. 'Ali', he called, 'get some food ready — a leg of mutton and a cup of milk — we are going to have a feast tonight. And you will invite all the sons of Abu al-Muttalib so that I can tell them what God has commanded me to say'.

'Ali quickly went about the preparations, but not without wondering secretly how a leg of mutton and a cup of milk would feed the 40 members of the Quraysh.

One by one the guests arrived. Old Abu Talib, Abu Sufyan, others of Muhammad's uncles, 'Abbas, Hamza — there must have been forty of them — seated themselves on cushions of hide. 'Ali placed the platter of mutton in the centre and each guest began to serve himself with great appetite. 'Ali could not believe his eyes, because as each generous portion of meat was devoured and the guests began to avail themselves of a second portion, the leg of mutton grew no smaller... there was no end to the amount of meat it provided! As the astonished youth prepared to remark on it, he raised his eyes and saw, on the other side of the gathering, the Prophet looking at him, smiling.

The end of the meal had come and the guests were relaxed and talking quietly to one another when the Prophet called for their attention. He spoke again of his mission as the Messenger of God. He warned them against the worship of idols and the other evil practices which they had fallen into. He implored them for their own sakes to turn to the One God so that they would be rewarded in the life to come. The pleasures of this life, he told them, would end with this life, whereas their good deeds would bring them eternal blessings.

Finally, the Prophet stood and raised his voice high and clear: 'Who will stand by me in my mission?' He looked around at each of them, and each in turn looked away.

In the awkward silence that followed, young 'Ali stepped forward, and taking his place beside the Prophet, exclaimed: 'Then I shall! I will be your helper, your partner, O Messenger of God!'

The Prophet responded by laying his hand on the young man's head. A burst of laughter greeted this announcement, a voice called out to Abu Talib: 'Eh, brother, will you now do homage to your own son?'

Abu Talib bit his lip in embarrassment, while Abu Sufyan and Hamza laughed heartily at the joke. Still laughing, the guests prepared to take their leave. But in the years to come, they were not to forget the Prophet's parting words: 'Here he is! Here is 'Ali, my helper, my companion!'

It seemed as if Muhammad had failed to bring his message to the Quraysh. Yet he was determined to try once again. This time he would make it clear that this was not some sort of dream, some story he had made up, but a true revelation from the One God. A true warning that they must turn away from idols and wrong doing before it was too late.

How could he make them listen?

There was only one way left that he knew of. Driven by his faith and his determination to save his people, he walked out of the city and began to climb Mount Safa. When he reached the top, he called out the traditional cry of danger. A call used by the people of Makka only when the city is threatened:

'WA SABAHA! WA SABAHA!'

Every man, woman and child in Makka heard the cry. In no time a large crowd had gathered, among them the forty men of the Quraysh.

The Messenger looked down at his relatives in their multi-coloured robes and turbans and greeted each man in turn. Then, raising his voice so that all could hear, he pronounced:

'O Kinsmen of the Quraysh! If I were to warn you that an army was advancing to attack you from beyond those hills, would you believe me?'

'Yes!', they answered. 'Most certainly!' they called back.

'Then listen, kinsmen. I have been commanded to

41

warn you that there is none worthy of worship but the One God; that a terrible fate awaits those of you who persist in worshipping idols. A terrible punishment indeed for the drinkers and gamblers, for those who bury their girl children alive, for those who steal from orphans. So bear witness with me that there is none but the One Almighty God...'

Suddenly, from the back of the assembly a voice like the slashing of steel cut the air.

'Liar!', it cried. Abu Lahab's face could be seen through the crowd, fiery with rage... for Lahab means flame... 'Liar!' he shouted again, trembling with fury. 'You dare disturb us in our work to listen to this nonsense?' And feverishly picking up stones, he hurled them in the direction of the Prophet.

'Ali and Zayd, who had not been standing far off, were dumbfounded. They watched Abu Lahab and Abu Jahl turn on their heels and walk off, while the rest of the crowd, confused and disturbed, followed them.

For a long while the Prophet stood pale and still. The blue vein in the middle of his forehead throbbed and swelled. Then he closed his eyes, drew his cloak around him and seemed to retire from the world.

Hours went by. Darkness had fallen while the Prophet, still enveloped in his mantle, sat in silence. It was later that the boys were to hear the prophetic words:

'Perish the Hands of Abu Lahab
Let him perish!
His wealth and his gains shall avail him not.'

9
The Opposition

Twilight was falling over the city of Makka. It was the hour when the evil forces of nature return to the bowels of the earth. Wild dogs howled mournfully in the distance. The winds caused the sand to be whipped up in angry spirals across the desert. The dying sun, hidden behind a bank of clouds, cast an eerie light over the Ka'ba, and on the group of men gathered there. They were the elders of the Quraysh clan. Abu Lahab, spitting out his words like date seeds, was holding forth on his favourite subject: his nephew Muhammad. The image of the god Hubal leered down at him from the entrance of the Ka'ba as he spoke.

'He is not just a dreamer and a fake, he is a dangerous mad-man! A man whose design it is to undermine the beliefs and traditions of generations! Do you not see where this will lead? If he manages to convince the people of Makka that their idols are worthless and succeeds in having them destroyed, who then, will come on pilgrimage? Makka will be empty of pilgrims and our coffers will be empty of gold... and we, kinsmen, shall be poor and miserable. Shall we suffer because of the follies of an arrogant imbecile?'

At this point Abu Jahl interrupted. His eyes narrowed to slits as he whispered, 'If you want my opinion, he should be slain! And, by Hubal', he added, 'I shall be happy to do the job'.

Another of the elders raised his hand to speak. His voice was measured and he spoke with a clever tongue. 'I am afraid, my dear Abu Jahl, that your violent methods have often resulted in the very opposite of what we are trying to achieve. Just the other day you were so intent on piling insults publicly on Muhammad that Hamza, our great hunter, felt obliged to defend him. He then became so caught up in his defence of Muhammad that before he or anyone else knew what was happening, he declared himself a believer in the One God and a follower of Muhammad... pledging him faithful and loyal support forever!'

'So there drops another of our Quraysh into the sands of foolishness, and all because you, Abu Jahl, will not restrain yourself.'

Turning to Abu Lahab, he continued, 'We understand very well your meaning. But there are other methods of dealing with the problem'.

'What other methods, pray tell?', retorted Abu Lahab. 'Abu Talib himself, though refusing to abandon our Gods and Goddesses, has pledged to protect Muhammad. Twice we have tried to reason with him, but he holds firm. And other members of the Hashimite branch are remaining loyal to Muhammad, whether they believe his rantings or not. The Quraysh are divided. The Hashimites are protecting Muhammad, leaving only our side in opposition.'

'It has not stopped at that', interrupted another elder, breathlessly. 'Can it be that you have not heard this most unbelievable and shocking piece of news? Our formidable 'Umar, whose frightening anger no one dares provoke, has himself joined Muhammad and his rebellious lot.'

Cries of disbelief came from all who were listening, but the elder continued: ' 'Umar discovered to his horror that his own sister and her husband had secretly joined the rebels, so in fury he went to their house, determined to chastise them firmly. But once there, I was told, he overheard the verses which Muhammad

44

had taught them; he then became so bewitched by these words, that in such a state, for it must have been madness... he proceeded to the house of Al-Arqam where Muhammad and his band were known to hold their meetings. Of course they all trembled at the sound of 'Umar's voice behind the door, but Muhammad, I was told, let him in and said to him, "How long, O 'Umar, will you continue with this persecution? Until some calamity befalls you?"

'And then to everyone's astonishment 'Umar replied, "I bear witness that there is but One God, and that you, Muhammad, are his Messenger".'

Upon hearing this, the elders groaned with dismay. 'We are lost without 'Umar's firm hand', cried one of them.

The clever elder spoke again. 'It is apparent that we have lost two strong men. Violence, however, can only lead to blood feuds... blood which in the end might be our own. I have said that there are other persuasive methods. If you would be so courteous as to listen... here is the plan. We shall cut off all sources of food from Muhammad and his followers. As the elders of the Quraysh and governing body of Makka we shall post a ban in the Ka'ba forbidding the sale of food to the rebels...'

'Or the sale of anything else!' added Abu Lahab excitedly.

'Yes anything else. No clothing. No goods whatsoever. Nor shall they be allowed to marry or carry out other transactions.'

'Starve them out!' shouted Abu Jahl. 'We shall see then how strong a hold this imposter has over them, for I doubt not that once their bellies cry out for food, their voices shall cry for Hubal and Al-Lat.'

'Right! Excellent! Excellent plan' agreed Abu Lahab and the others.

All present struck hands in agreement. The elder, whose idea it was, proceeded to write up the ban, enclose it in a sheepskin envelope, and having sealed it, posted it high in the Ka'ba. This done they went their various ways through the dark streets.

For two long years the ban remained posted in the Ka'ba. For two long years the Prophet Muhammad and his followers suffered poverty, boycott and starvation. Their misery was alleviated only by the mercy of a few who taking pity occasionally smuggled small supplies of food to the district where they had taken refuge.

Despite great hunger and poverty, the Believers remained loyal to Muhammad and his message. Seated in the quarters granted them by the faithful Abu Talib, they prayed in the way the Prophet had taught them. They gathered around him cross-legged on mats of palm and listened to his advice or asked him questions. Some were privileged to be present when he received the words of revelation and repeated them aloud, whereupon they would quickly write them down on old pieces of sheepskin or date leaves or whatever they could find handy.

These later formed part of what are called the Makkan Suras of the Glorious Quran.

Through the long night vigils, when the world outside was quiet, the Prophet Muhammad could hear his followers reciting these Suras and learning them by heart. From a corner of the house, a deep voice chanted in sonorous Arabic:

'...And they have commanded
No more than this:
To worship God
Offering Him sincere devotion
Being true in faith
To establish regular prayer

46

And practice regular charity
And that is the religion
Right and Straight...'

and in another corner, a young and vibrant voice rang
out:

'In the name of God, Most Gracious, Most
Merciful.
Say: God is One
The One and Only
He begets not, nor is he begotten
And there is none like unto Him.'

Then, as the dawn light appeared over Makka, they
joined the Prophet in prayer.

Now one of Muhammad's relatives (who was not
under the ban) called Hisham, became very upset.
How could members of his own family be allowed to
starve like stray dogs? He was going to do something
about it. Late one night he loaded up his camel with all
sorts of food and provisions and sneaked down a dark
street to the alley leading to the Believers' quarters.
Now how was he going to persuade that camel to go
down the alley without actually breaking the ban, he
asked himself. There was only one way to do that.
Stepping back, he gave his camel a big whack on the
side, and down the alley it went, very obediently. This
worked for a while, but it was no solution. He had had
enough of it. Gathering four other men who were in
agreement with him, they met secretly outside Makka,
with the intention of dissolving the ban.

'Are you content that they should perish while we
just look on agreeing with it? You will find that the
Quraysh will do the same to you' he warned.

The next day at the Ka'ba one of the five men who
had been with Hisham the night before spoke while

circling the Ka'ba:

'Oh people of Makka, are we to eat and clothe ourselves while the others perish? By God I will not sit down until this evil boycotting document is torn up!

But Abu Jahl had overheard him. 'You lie! It shall not be torn up!' he cackled.

'You are a greater liar! We do not hold with what is written, we never did hold with it. We want nothing more to do with the ban.'

Abu Jahl pointed an evil finger at him. 'You decided this before! You discussed this somewhere else!' he accused.

But Hisham paid no attention. He stepped forward and reached out for the ban. But as he went to tear it down, he found that little white ants had already eaten it, and nothing was left of the evil ban save the words:

IN THE NAME OF ALLAH

The days of the ban were over. Muhammad and his followers were once again allowed to circulate through Makka, to buy and sell as before.

10
The Jinn

The Prophet Muhammad, accompanied by Zayd and
'Ali, walked swiftly through the streets of Makka. His
body leaned slightly forward, as if he were climbing a
hill, his hands were clasped behind him. Now that the
ban had been lifted, the Believers could wander freely
in the city and join the gatherings and fairs. There, the
Prophet would speak to groups of travellers or anyone
who was willing to listen: some were curious to hear his
message, but more often than not, the rasping voice of
Abu Lahab, who never tired of dogging his footsteps,
would interrupt.

One day, as they approached the Hajj fair, a group
of travellers stopped the Prophet. A youth, dressed in a
striped Yemeni garment, said to him: 'You who are
called the Messenger of God, what harm, tell us, could
befall us if we refuse to listen to you?' The Prophet
began to speak to them of the Day of Judgement, and
quoted one of the Suras:

> 'On that day will men
> come forth in companies sorted out
> to be shown the Deeds
> that they have done.
>
> Then, shall anyone who
> has done an atom's weight of good
> see it!
>
> And anyone who,
> has done an atom's weight
> of evil, shall see it.'

وَإِذْ صَرَفْنَآ إِلَيْكَ نَفَرًا مِّنَ الْجِنِّ يَسْتَمِعُونَ الْقُرْآنَ

فَلَمَّا حَضَرُوهُ قَالُوٓا أَنْصِتُوا فَلَمَّا قُضِىَ وَلَّوْا إِلَى

قَوْمِهِمْ مُنْذِرِينَ ۞ قَالُوا يَا قَوْمَنَآ إِنَّا سَمِعْنَا كِتَابًا

أُنْزِلَ مِنْ بَعْدِ مُوسَى مُصَدِّقًا لِّمَا بَيْنَ يَدَيْهِ يَهْدِىٓ

إِلَى الْحَقِّ وَإِلَى طَرِيقٍ مُّسْتَقِيمٍ ۞ يَا قَوْمَنَآ أَجِيبُوا دَاعِىَ

اللهِ وَآمِنُوا بِهِ يَغْفِرْ لَكُمْ مِّنْ ذُنُوبِكُمْ وَيُجِرْكُمْ مِّنْ

عَذَابٍ أَلِيمٍ ۞ وَمَنْ لَّا يُجِبْ دَاعِىَ اللهِ فَلَيْسَ بِمُعْجِزٍ

فِى الْأَرْضِ وَلَيْسَ لَهُ مِنْ دُونِهِ أَوْلِيَآءُ أُولَئِكَ فِى

﴾ ضَلَالٍ مُّبِينٍ ۞ ﴿

29. Behold, We turned
    Towards thee a company
    Of Jinns (quietly) listening
    To the Qur-ān: when they
    Stood in the presence
    Thereof, they said. 'Listen
    In silence!' When the (reading)
    Was finished, they returned
    To their people, to warn
    (Them of their sins).

30. They said, 'O our people!
    We have heard a Book
    Revealed after Moses,
    Confirming what came
    Before it: it guides (men)
    To the Truth and
    To a Straight Path.

31. 'O our people, hearken
    To the one who invites
    (You) to God, and believe
    in him: He will forgive
    You your faults,
    And deliver you from
    A Penalty Grievous.

32. 'If any does not hearken
    To the one who invites
    (Us) to God, he cannot
    Frustrate (God's Plan) on earth,
    And no protectors can he have
    Besides God: such men
    (Wander) in manifest error.'

    (Sūra 46 Al-Aḥqāf 29—32)

51

Just then, as so often happened, the lean body of Abu Lahab pushed its way to where the group was standing: 'Do not believe his lies!' he cried. 'He is mad!' The travellers fell back and went their ways, not wishing to be involved in unpleasantness.

Further on, another group of men who were versed in the Scriptures and Holy Books stopped the Believers and addressed the Prophet: 'You call yourself a Messenger of God', they said, 'but messengers of God in the past have always performed miracles... Jesus could raise men from the dead and Moses could turn a rod into a snake or hold back the sea.' The Prophet turned towards them and said simply, 'The miracle is this: the revelation of the Quran'.

As they walked on, the Messenger placed his hand on 'Ali's shoulder, 'It is true that the prophets Moses and Jesus performed miracles, but for all that, there were still many who did not believe.'

Just as they reached the house, they met with an angry crowd, who began jeering at them and shouting insults: 'Profaner of our Gods!' — 'Troublemaker, idiot!' One of them, giving a yell, seized a clod of dirt and threw it at the Prophet's head.

Fatima, the Prophet's daughter, who had seen what had happened, quickly brought the Prophet into the house, cleansed his head with loving gestures and began to weep.

'Do not weep, my daughter... for you shall see, your father has God for a protector' the Prophet told her.

In the house, the Prophet called his dear friend Abu Bakr to his side and began talking with him:

'My dearest wife, my comforter in distress, Khadija is dead, and Abu Talib, my protector, is also lain to rest. Our little company of Believers in the One God is strong in their faith, but the community does not grow in this city. I wonder, dear friend, what direction we should follow.'

Young Zayd who had overheard the Prophet's words and could not bear another's distress, searched within himself for words of encouragement, and hit upon an idea.

'Oh Messenger of God', he said, approaching, 'I have heard of a town not far off... a lovely town where fruit trees grow and water flows, where the air is cool and pleasant... could we not go there and seek for men who will believe in the Faith?'

The Messenger smiled and drew Zayd to him. 'You speak of Taif, my son. Yes, there remains Taif. Shall we go there, you and I? It is a long journey, but with God's help we will make it.'

That is how the Prophet and his adopted son, Zayd, started on their long fifty mile trek up to the Garden City of Taif.

Left alone, Abu Bakr shook his head, 'We no longer have Abu Talib's protection'. He thought to himself, 'For our Messenger to venture forth is a most dangerous thing to do'.

Having finally arrived in beautiful Taif, Muhammad, accompanied by Zayd, immediately went to see the three brothers, chiefs of the town. But it soon became apparent that they were not at all impressed by the Prophet's words.

'Hah!' replied one of them. 'You are supposed to be sent by God? I'd sooner tear up the covering of the Ka'ba than believe that!'

The second one looked the Prophet up and down. 'Couldn't God have found somebody more suitable than you for a Prophet?' he sneered.

The third one backed away and rolled his eyes, 'By god, if you're telling the truth and you really are a Prophet, then you're too important for me to speak to...

and if you're not a Prophet and you're lying... then you're not fit to have a conversation with!'

All the people who had come to hear Muhammad talking to their chiefs became angry, and although the Messenger tried again to explain his mission to them, they became violent, jeering and yelling insults, and finally ran after the Prophet and Zayd, pelting them with anything they could find, stones and clods of dirt. Muhammad and Zayd, who had been wounded in the leg and was limping, stumbled down the rocky slopes till they came to a vineyard. There they stopped to rest, and the owner, taking pity on them, sent water with which they could wash their wounds, and offered them fresh grapes from his vines.

On their long journey back to Makka, they stopped again in the Valley of Nakhla. Zayd then left the Prophet behind, while he went on ahead to Makka. Having been granted protection by Ibn Adi, who offered his house as a place of refuge, he returned to the deserted valley.

It was nightfall when he reached there, the time of day when the Jinn, both good and evil, frequent lonely places. He expected to find the Prophet exhausted and discouraged, but instead he found him radiant and smiling. Zayd, who could not understand the reason for this, asked: 'Is all well with the Messenger of God?'

'Praise God, all is well', responded the Prophet. 'For if the men of Taif have not listened to the truth, there are others who have.' And then the Prophet began to recite:

> 'Say: It has been
> revealed to me that
> a company of jinn
> listened to the Quran.
> They said "We have

54

really heard a wonderful recital!
It gives guidance
to the Right
and we have believed therein.
We shall not join in worship
Any God with our Lord".'

11
The Night Journey

'We were not present, Abu Bakr, when the Prophet told of the Night Journey, so we have come to ask you to recount it to us', asked one among a crowd of Believers who had gathered at his door.

'Yes, we beseech you, Abu Bakr, do tell us what wondrous things took place', said another.

'They say God has blessed His Prophet... and has blessed us all...' said a third.

'Come in, come in, all of you and be most welcome', answered Abu Bakr. 'The blessings of God be upon you. I shall tell you the story as best I can, for we were so elated upon hearing it that it is possible — God forgive me for this — that I may slip up somewhere along in the telling.'

Having spoken, Abu Bakr then seated himself in the middle of the room so all could hear, and others took their places crosslegged on the mats, making room for as many as possible in the small space. The voices died down to a whisper; a reverent hush fell over the gathering. Abu Bakr began a prayer: 'All praise to the One God for what we are about to recount...'

Suddenly, the door burst open. In the doorway stood the familiar figure of 'Abbas, his eyes alight and turban slightly askew.

'Well now, what's this I hear?' he bellowed cheerfully. 'My nephew's camel has sprouted wings and flown to Jerusalem in the middle of the night? This promises to be a good yarn, and I would not miss it for the world! Things have been too dreary around here for too long: so get on with it!' He pushed his way to the front of the room. 'And make it lively while you're about it.'

'Abbas was a Believer in his own way, and that was, when he felt like it.

'The Prophet's camel did not sprout wings', retorted Abu Bakr with dignity. 'Now, if we have all settled down and are prepared to listen quietly...' he said, his eyes upon 'Abbas, 'I shall continue'.

Abu Bakr lifted his eyes a moment, and then began: 'The Prophet, that night, was very tired from the long walks and harrassment he had during the day, so he slept very soundly. Suddenly a voice called him so insistently that he woke up, and there before him stood Gabriel in full splendour. Gabriel beckoned for him to follow and when they reached the doorway, presented him with a most marvellous beast such as has never been seen on earth: a dazzling white mare with a human face; its wings were like those of an eagle, but even more enormous; the span of its hoofs reached as far as the eye could see — it could travel even faster than light. ''This is Burraq'', the angel told our Messenger, and bade him mount the mare. Off they flew into the night sky leaving Makka far behind.

'All along this journey they beheld many strange and terrible sights — too numerous to be told here. Some were designed to tempt the Prophet and lead him away from the true path, others were examples of the terrible punishments which man brings upon himself as a result of the sins he commits on earth.

'When they were over the city of Jerusalem, Gabriel ordered Burraq to begin the descent. They landed at the gates of the temple, and there the Messenger tied Burraq to a ring, just as the Prophets of old had done. The Messenger of God then entered the temple, and there he saw Jesus and Moses, and many other prophets besides. And let me add that our Messenger described each one to us so that we fancied we could see him. Having prayed in the temple with the others, our Prophet came out, and he beheld another wondrous thing. Reaching all the way up into the heavens was a Ladder of Light. Gabriel told him to mount the Ladder, and he did so, as quickly and as easily as if it had been made of air.

'They ascended until they came to the First Heaven. Gabriel knocked at the gate. "Who is there?" they were asked from within. "Gabriel." "And who is with you?" "Muhammad." "Has he received his mission?" "He has." "Then he is welcome!" and the gate was opened.

'Inside the First Heaven, all appeared to be of silver. There were stars suspended on chains of gold and within each star was an angel, placed as a sentinel to guard against demons who might try to enter. They met with an old man, whom Gabriel introduced as Adam, and he greeted our Messenger most warmly. All around were animals of every shape and size. These animals, Adam explained, are in reality angels who intercede with God on behalf of the animals on earth. In their midst stood a huge white rooster whose crowing awakens the seven heavens, and shall continue to do so until Judgement Day.

'Bidding farewell to Adam, Gabriel and the Prophet proceeded to the Second Heaven. When they received permission to enter, they found themselves in a place which seemed made of polished steel. Noah was there and came to greet them, and if I am not mistaken, Jesus and John the Baptist were there also.

'On they went to the Third Heaven — a huge abode, decorated with myriads of precious stones too brilliant for human eyes to endure. Before him the Prophet saw an angel of stupendous size whose eyes were 70,000 days' journey apart. He had at his command one hundred thousand soldier-angels, all armed. He did not look up as they approached. In front of him a vast book was spread open in which he was continually writing and blotting out. "This, O Muhammad, is Azrail, the Angel of Death. For each name he writes, a person is born; and for each name blotted out, a man's time is come and he must die".

'Mounting to the Fourth Heaven, they met with other angels; the height of one of these was five hundred days' journey in length. Seeing him, the Prophet asked, "Why does he weep?" "He is the Angel of Tears", responded Gabriel. "He predicts the evils which befall mankind, and weeps for mankind."

'Arriving at the Fifth Heaven, the Prophet was greeted by Aaron, the brother of Moses, and was warmly welcomed. But in this Heaven stood the most hideous sight of all — an angel whose face was copper-coloured and disfigured with warts. His eyes flashed lightning and he carried a flaming lance. Bright coals burned in front of him and a mound of red-hot chains glowed at his feet. "This", said Gabriel, "is the Angel of Divine Vengeance. His duty is to punish with a terrible punishment all those who deny their Creator, and all those who commit grievous sins against themselves and their fellow creatures".

'Leaving this terrible sight, Muhammad and Gabriel reached the Sixth Heaven, where, as before, they announced themselves and were granted permission to enter. The Sixth Heaven was composed of Hasala stone, which is like the carbuncle. And here, the Prophet beheld the strangest sight of all. Here stood an angel whose form was half fire, half snow. Yet the snow did not melt, nor was the fire extinguished. Around him were hordes of angels proclaiming in song: "Glory to the Most High who has united snow and fire! May he

60

unite all his faithful servants in obedience to His law". "This is the guardian angel of Heaven and Earth" explained Gabriel. "It is he who visits the nations and calls certain people amongst them to the service of God: And so shall he continue until the Resurrection."

'In the Sixth Heaven, our Messenger met with Moses again, who welcomed him and wept, saying "Here is a Prophet who will call more of his nation to the service of God than ever I was able to".

'Finally, they reached the Seventh Heaven which was filled with a wondrous light never yet beheld by human eyes. There the Prophet saw many marvellous things, among which was an angel larger than the earth in magnitude. He had 70,000 tongues speaking 70,000 languages, all chanting praises to the Creator.

'Suddenly Muhammad was transported still higher, and there he saw the Lote Tree, or the tree of heaven whose branches extend wider than the distance between the sun and the earth. Myriads of angels rejoice beneath its shade and from it issue four rivers, two which flow into Paradise and two to the earth below.

'From there, the Prophet entered the House of Adoration, visited by the 70,000 angels of the highest order, who make their holy circuit around it. Our Prophet was then brought into the realm of the Holy Abode; which no words can describe, although our Prophet did say that a sweet fragrance prevailed all around him, and that he felt the touch of an invisible hand on his shoulder and chest, which produced a feeling of unspeakable happiness. It was here, the Prophet told us, that he received the laws of our religion, which is called Islam, and which means surrender to the One God.

'Upon his descent from the Heavenly Abode, our Prophet met again with Moses. "How many prayers a day were prescribed for your religion?" asked Moses. "Fifty prayers a day", responded our Messenger. Moses was troubled.

'"How do you imagine, Muhammad, that your people will pray fifty times a day? You may believe me, for I have had experience in this matter, and people are quite incapable of carrying out such an instruction. Go back — go back and ask for a smaller number."

'And so our Prophet did return, and ask for fewer prayers to be prescribed. On his way back down, he met with Moses again, who asked him: "How many prayers are prescribed to you now?" "Forty" replied the Prophet.."Forty! Impossible! Go back and ask for fewer." And so the situation continued: Our Prophet obtaining that the number of prayers be reduced, and Moses insisting that it be reduced still further, until finally, Moses said: "How many this time?" "Five prayers a day" our Messenger answered. "That is still too much. Imagine an ordinary man praying five times a day! Return again!"

'"No", answered our Messenger, "I have returned too many times and I am ashamed". And so saying, he bade Moses farewell and began his descent.

'Down they went, Gabriel and our Prophet, by way of the Ladder of Light, till they reached the temple in Jerusalem, and when they reached it, they found Burraq, whom they unfastened. Back they flew to the house where Gabriel had found the Prophet sleeping. Looking up at the sky, our Messenger was most surprised to see the first rays of morning light appearing. His journey to Jerusalem, to the realms Above, and back again, had taken almost no time.

'Abu Bakr', asked one in the group, 'Was there no mention of vessels of wine and milk?'

'Ah yes indeed, (you see how easily one forgets). Yes, the Angel Gabriel presented our Messenger with two vessels, one containing milk, and the other wine. The Prophet took the vessel of milk and drank from it. "You have rightly chosen" Gabriel told him. "Had you drunk the other, your people might have gone astray."'

'Abbas raised his eyebrows. 'Well, what of the wine? Who drank that?' he asked, but no one paid any attention to him for they were rendered dazed and speechless by the story they had just heard.

In the name of God, Most Gracious, Most Merciful.

1. Glory to (God)
   Who did take His Servant
   For a Journey by night
   From the Sacred Mosque
   To the Farthest Mosque,
   Whose precincts We did
   Bless, — in order that We
   Might show him some
   Of Our Signs: for He
   Is the One Who heareth
   And seeth (all things).   (Sūra 17 Al-Isrā' 1)

64

12
The Cave

Makka was bustling with tribes from all over Arabia as the month of yearly pilgrimage came to a close. Proud Bedouin Arabs with their proud camels had come from the West. The Bani Dhakwan and the idolaters from Taif were offering elaborate sacrifices to their goddess Al-Lat. The Bani Hawazin and the Bani Amir had completed the circular ritual around the Ka'ba and were heading northwards to the desert. As night fell on the city, the Makkan merchants, like fat cats, their purses bursting with gold, returned to the comforts of their homes.

Meanwhile, 'Abbas, who had done pretty well for himself, invited the Prophet and his companions to his home for a celebration. It had been a long time since the Believers had tasted such a feast.

'Bring me my Oud', called out 'Abbas when the food had been cleared away, 'and I'll sing you a ballad that will wipe the wrinkles off a dried raisin. Mind you join in the chorus'.

Suddenly, the merriment was interrupted by a sharp knock at the door. 'Abbas hastened to answer, and cries of welcome greeted the newcomer. 'Ali and Zayd did not recognise him at first. He was not dressed in Makkan tunic and his manner was almost frantic. He glanced furtively behind him as the door closed, and examined the faces of those present as if to assure himself there were no enemies. The Prophet, observing this, signalled for the companions to retire to another room, and sent 'Ali and Zayd to fetch fresh milk and a platter of dates.

'Who is he? Where is he from?' whispered Zayd.

'It's Mus'ab, don't you remember?' answered 'Ali. 'Last year, after the pilgrimage, our Messenger sent him to Madina along with seven new Believers who were returning home. He has remained in that city all year, teaching them the prayers and the Sacred Verses. And now, here he is back in Makka.'

When Zayd and 'Ali returned with the tray of dates, Mus'ab was speaking urgently in a low voice:

'They are ready to meet with God's Messenger tonight at midnight, in the glen of 'Aqaba... seventy Believers from Madina!'

'Seventy? I'd heard there were only seven', interrupted 'Abbas.

'God be praised, now there are seventy. They wish to offer their homes and protection to God's Messenger and to the Believers from Makka.'

'Praise be to God, whose intervention comes at the most unexpected times' exclaimed the Prophet. 'May God reward you, Mus'ab, for all you have done.' Muhammad rose and wrapped his cloak about him. 'And now, Uncle, I ask your permission to leave. It is late and it would be dangerous to keep these valiant followers waiting.'

'Not so fast!' interrupted 'Abbas. 'I will not allow you to go sauntering off alone in the dead of night to that godforsaken and dangerous place. You need a strong and courageous and sensible person to accompany you, and I,' he added, preening his whiskers, 'am that person! I insist on going with you.'

The Prophet smiled. 'Very well, Uncle,' he said, 'but it would be best for this meeting to take place in utmost secrecy, for we must in no way jeopardise their safety. Therefore', he added, looking at Zayd and 'Ali, 'I shall ask that no one else be allowed to accompany us'.

A half moon was shining over the hills of 'Aqaba. As the clouds, one by one covered its brightness, dark figures, one at a time, hurried down the slopes of the hills to the glen. Finally, a group of seventy had joined the Prophet and his uncle. 'Abbas then raised his hand and called for attention.

'O People of Madina!' he announced. 'Take care what you do! You have undertaken a dangerous responsibility. Many of my nephew's followers have been persecuted. Some have been tortured and killed, others have fled to Abyssinia. If you offer asylum to my nephew and the Believers, even your countrymen may turn against you. And all of Makka will be up in arms. But if, in spite of this, you are resolved to defend Muhammad, then give the pledge! If you are uncertain, leave now while there is still time.'

"Abbas', responded a young chief from Madina, 'as surely as we stand here, our decision remains firm. Speak then, O Messenger of God, that we may at last hear your words!'

The moment awaited so long had come. The Prophet came forward to speak. A hush fell over the assembly as the beautiful Arabic verses of the Glorious Quran resounded through the darkness, touching the fellings of all who listened:

'In the name of God, the Compassionate, the Merciful:
Praise be to God, Lord of Creation
Most gracious, most merciful
Master of the Day of Judgement
Thee alone do we worship
And to Thee alone we pray for help
Guide us to the straight path
The path of those whom Thou hast favoured...
Who have not incurred wrath
And who go not astray.'

67

These and other verses were recited by the Prophet, after which he asked the assembly if they would be willing to protect and defend him in case of strife.

All rose to their feet: 'We swear to defend thee, O Messenger of God!' they declared in one voice.

'Hush! Quiet!' whispered 'Abbas Ibn Ubada as loudly as he could. 'Do you think the hills and the jinn and the creatures of the desert have no ears? If you wish to pledge your loyalty, then come forward, each one of you and strike hands over the bargain... and no more shouting, I say!'

Seventy Helpers from Madina, as the Prophet now called them, stepped forward one by one to strike hands and repeat the pledge. But just as the last one presented himself, a voice arose from beyond the hill, a wail, like that of a wild beast:

'People of Makka! Beware! Muhammad the Mad seeks to defy you!'

The Believers gasped and stood trembling, but the Prophet's deep voice broke the terror in their hearts: 'Fear him not!' he admonished. 'It is but the Demon of 'Aqaba, the enemy of God. Fear him not!'

The people of Madina, then, cautiously began to return to their tents. From the last group of men, a bold youth stepped forward and asked of the Prophet: 'What do you promise as a reward, O Messenger of God, if we should die for the cause?'

The Prophet turned and faced him, 'Paradise!' he replied. And on this last word, they disappeared up the dark slopes of 'Aqaba.

The Demon of 'Aqaba lost no time in doing mischief. By the very next night the Elders of the Quraysh, who had somehow heard of the Pledge, gathered in the Ka'ba to discuss the matter.

'He plans to flee to Madina taking all his supporters

69

with him'... announced one. 'Surely he will round up an army against us!'

'Banish him! Banish him now, to the wilderness!' suggested a second.

'Let him be walled up as in a tomb, and fed through a crevice till he perishes' cried another.

'No, kinsmen!' cried Abu Jahl. 'By Hubal, there is only one permanent way to rid ourselves of him forever. Only one permanent way...' his eyes narrowed to slits as he fingered the golden hilt of his scimitar.

Abu Sufyan nodded in agreement. Another exclaimed: 'Murder? Commit the murder of a kinsman? Never will any one of us agree to such a thing!'

'Of course not!' snarled Abu Jahl. 'No *one* of us would dare commit such an act... but *together* we shall do it! Who, then, will bear the guilt? Does not each one of you possess a blade such as this one?' he said, unsheathing the shiny steel of his scimitar. 'And are we not all able to thrust together... thus!' he demonstrated, slashing the air with ferocity.

The assembly hesitated, then nodded in unspoken agreement, while clasping the hilts of their scimitars.

Behind them, a voice broke their silence: 'O men of Makka! Thrust, thrust together!' it whined. But when they turned to look, they saw but an old man from a distant tribe.

Muhammad the Prophet sat up suddenly on his mat in the dark room. What had awakened him? Was it Gabriel? Certainly there was no angel here now. The silence was oppressive with a foreboding of evil; the very air reeked of danger. Drawing his cloak about him, the Prophet sat absolutely still and listened. Seconds later he heard behind the walls a shuffling of feet and muffled voices. A prayer of protection formed silently on his lips, for he had guessed the intention of those lurking outside the house.

70

Quickly then the Prophet awakened 'Ali, who lay close by and gave him his cloak which 'Ali took, and covering himself with it, lay down on the Prophet's mat.

Within moments, the Prophet had miraculously slipped past the awaiting assassins and disappeared into the night, towards the home of Abu Bakr.

Outside the house, a Quraysh youth peered between the shutters and spied 'Ali's form covered with the Prophet's green cloak.

'Muhammad is there, asleep', he whispered.

'At dawn', responded the other, his teeth clenched in determination, 'at dawn, when he steps out that door, we shall silence him forever'.

'Ali lay motionless on the mat, his head drenched in sweat, waiting and listening. A long time seemed to pass; no sound broke the silence of the night. They had set a trap, they had planned a murder, but by God's grace, they had failed.

Dawn broke over Makka. The band of assassins crept silently out of the shadows towards the front of the house. A door swung open, their scimitars flashed upwards, then stopped abruptly in mid air. An astonished cry of disappointment escaped their lips.

In the doorway, his head held high, his shoulders squared, stood 'Ali. His black eyes searched deeply into those of each man standing before him. Then, tossing the Prophet's green cloak over his arm, he pushed past the drawn scimitars and marched down the road towards the Ka'ba.

The Prophet, with Abu Bakr at his side, stumbled up the rocky slopes to the caves outside Makka. Had they taken camels and followed the road to Madina, they surely would have been caught. As it was, the assassins, discovering their error, had turned in the direction of the caves and were now close behind them.

Like the Prophet, Abu Bakr was exhausted, thirsty and covered with dust. Abu Bakr had been so anxious to accompany the Prophet to Madina... to join the others who had already left... but never under conditions such as these! 'How is such a thing possible?' he asked himself as they scrambled up the sharp rocky slopes on their hands and knees. 'A Messenger of God, driven out of his own home... hunted on foot like a wild beast... and by members of his own clan? Surely the world has gone mad! May God protect us from harm!' he gasped aloud.

'Courage, Abu Bakr, God will hear you', answered the Prophet.

They reached the caves a little before nightfall, and took refuge in one of them. Close behind they could hear the horsemen of the Quraysh calling to each other. Abu Bakr scrambled as far back as he could into the cave while the Prophet closed his eyes in prayer.

The sound of hooves slipping over dry gravel and rock grew nearer. The Quraysh were not far from the mouth of the cave, and were dismounting. Abu Bakr held his breath in mounting anxiety.

'In the cave, they must be in the cave —,this way!' cried a voice.

Tears came to Abu Bakr's eyes. All was lost. God's own Messenger would be slain, and he along with him.

'What shall we do?' exclaimed Abu Bakr, trembling. 'There are but two of us!'

'You are mistaken, brother,' replied the Prophet, 'there are three of us. You, I and Almighty God'.

By this time the footsteps had come right to the entrance of the cave. Abu Bakr shut his eyes tightly and prayed.

'By Hubal, they *can't* be in this one', called a voice at the entrance. 'It's covered with branches and spiderwebs. No one has been here since Muhammad was born!'

'Over to the north slopes, then... this way!' answered a voice further off.

The sounds of hooves and voices became fainter. The men had gone. Abu Bakr, still too terrified to move, praised God in his heart. Then he remembered, suddenly, the man's words. Branches? Spiderwebs? Slowly he opened his eyes. The cave did not look the same at all. Over the entrance a spider had spun its web from one side of the opening to the other, and was swinging, now, from its silver thread. Above it, a branch hung low, with a nest couched amidst its leaves. In the nest, a grey dove was singing peacefully.

Abu Bakr rubbed his eyes and looked again. The Prophet was watching the spider spin a last silver thread to complete its web.

'O Messenger of God, how can this be?' exclaimed Abu Bakr.

He received no answer, save for the cooing of the dove. The Prophet turned to Abu Bakr and smiled.

Every night, for three long nights, Abu Bakr's little daughter cautiously led her camel across the desert to the caves, bringing food and drink to the fugitives; and every morning a faithful follower drove his herd by the entrance to wipe out all traces of her visit.

The news they heard from Makka was disturbing. 'O Messenger of God', said Abu Bakr, sighing. 'They are offering a reward of one hundred camels for your capture'.

The Prophet closed his eyes and leaned back against the wall of the cave. 'One hundred camels for your capture.' Drifting back in time, he recalled days long gone. A little boy, wrapped in his grandfather's great warm cloak... late at night in the Ka'ba... listening to an old man's story... his grandfather's voice... 'One

73

hundred camels for the life of my son' he had said.
'One hundred camels...'

Out of the darkness the dove's song announced the
coming dawn. Rousing himself, the Prophet called to
Abu Bakr, and together they began the morning prayer:

> '...I seek refuge
> With the Lord of Dawn,
> From the mischief
> of Created things,
> From the mischief
> of darkness as it overspreads;
> From the mischief
> of those who practice
> Secret Arts;
> And from the mischief
> of the Envious One
> As he practices his envy.'

13
Madina

Her name was Al-Qaswa, and she was no ordinary
camel. She was an intelligent beast, and in the family of
animals, intelligent ones know full well which of their
kind are valued and which are not.

Her hide was almost white, and that was a rare
thing to see in a camel. Her double eyelashes were
thicker and fuller than most, giving her an air of elegant
dignity when she swung her long neck forwards and
back. Her gait, when slow, was as gracefully rhythmic
as the blue waves beating against the shore; and when
she ran, her feet, like plump cushions, carried her rider
over the sands with the swiftness of a doe. Al-Qaswa
was no ordinary camel, and what's more, she was the
Prophet's favourite.

After three nights in the cave, the Prophet and Abu
Bakr were finally on their way. Hearing that the
Quraysh had begun to give up the chase, Abu Bakr's
son had brought them two camels, smuggled out of
Makka during the night, and provisions which his sister
had prepared for the journey.

'God be praised!' cried Abu Bakr, weeping with
happiness. 'To Madina... at last!'

Who would have guessed it, to see those two
ragged travellers making their way across the arid
mountains, that their journey to Madina would be
remembered for all time? That in the future, the
calendar of every Believer around the world would
date from that very day.

Al-Qaswa knew for certain it was no ordinary

journey. This was not the usual route to Madina. Where were the landmarks, the oasis? Why were they following unbeaten paths along the sea? No birds flew their way, no lizards could be seen and no stops had been made except for the times of prayer.

Once they met with a single caravan from which they had obtained food and drink and fresh white garments from Syria. Then on they went, this way and that, by devious trails till they came to the oasis of Quba, close to Madina.

Unbeknown to the travellers, their arrival had been seen from far off, and the news had been passed on to the Believers in Madina who came each day to the point of lookout and searched the horizon for signs of their Prophet.

'He has come' they shouted from the lookout. 'The Prophet has come.' The news spread quickly and in no time at all, the Believers were racing down the streets of Madina, crowding around the Prophet and Abu Bakr and cheering with joy. 'Our Prophet is here' sang the children as they reached for the camel's reins and took turns stroking al-Qaswa's velvet nose.

The Prophet returned their welcome with his warm smile. 'Here is how you can show your joy', he said to the Believers. 'Give your neighbours the Salaam of Peace, bring food to the poor, stay close in feeling to your brothers, and offer up prayers while others sleep. And that is how you shall reach Paradise...'

For three days the weary travellers rested in Quba, accepting graciously the gifts of honey and dates and skins of milk that were offered. There, the Prophet laid the foundations for the very first mosque, or place of worship. There he gave his first sermon out in the open for all to hear.

Then on they went to Madina... and what a procession it was! Hamza the Hunter and mighty

'Umar strode along like giants through the crowd of Believers. Waving bows and scimitars, they cheered and shouted. 'We shall defend the Prophet with our lives'. Behind them followed the Chiefs of the city, clad in holiday raiments and glittering armour.

On marched the parade, through the gardens and palm groves of Madina, Al-Qaswa proudly bearing the Prophet, led them all. Beside her waved the Prophet's black banner, hastily made from a long turban mounted on a lance.

Amidst the joy and celebration the Prophet turned and called the cavalcade to a halt. While all waited in silence, the Prophet dismounted. Leaning down, he spread a cloth in the dust. He stood again calling aloud, 'God is Most Great', then bowing his head to the ground he completed the prayer of thanks to the One God, while the procession waited.

The Prophet, having mounted again, resumed the march, but at each step people along the way pleaded: 'Stay in my home, Oh Messenger' — 'Honour my house, O Prophet of God', so that the Prophet was obliged to halt and acknowledge their pleas.

Everyone gathered around. Whose house would the Prophet choose? What was he saying?

Al-Qaswa then raised her proud head. She had understood this much: the Prophet had spoken her name. She felt the reins go slack on her neck, and noticed that the eyes of all the men, women and children were staring only at her. This surprised even Al-Qaswa. What were they expecting her to do? Regaining her dignity she took a step forward, then two, and proceeded without direction from her master to find her own way down the streets. Behind her, the procession followed silently.

No reins were leading her, yet she seemed to be led. So she continued, hesitating, then moving along, till she came to a plot of land upon which was a date barn. There she stopped and fell to her knees.

From the neighbouring house the people rushed forward to welcome the Prophet. 'Umar announced then: 'Here shall the Prophet build his mosque and his home, and with these people shall he stay'.

Everyone cheered, and if some were disappointed they certainly didn't show it. One could never be sure who had led the camel to this spot and besides, as everyone knew, Al-Qaswa was no ordinary camel.

Never before had the people of Madina seen such a happy crowd at work. The noise and the singing could be heard all over the town. Children and old men stopped on their way home to watch the building of the mosque, and were surprised by what they saw. Where were the slaves and the labourers? These were the Helpers of Madina, and the Emigrants from Makka along with them, toiling and sweating in the dust, and most surprising of all, there was the Prophet himself, cutting and hauling bricks from one spot to another. They watched as 'Umar laid the foundation stones; along with him worked 'Ali and Zayd who had just arrived from Makka with their families.

They watched as Hamza directed the work. 'Save them for the roof', he shouted to Abu Bakr, who was cutting palm branches, 'the trunks will support them'.

Then, in the midst of everything, they burst into song:

'Joy, O Lord will surely come
When this earthly life is done —
Grant thy Mercy on us, Lord,
Emigrants and Helpers all!'

'Ali, who had spied someone lazing around, sang his own verse:

'The Prophet works and toils you see,
So don't just loaf under that tree.'

Again the chorus swelled forth:

'Joy, O Lord will surely come
When this earthly life is done...'

Then the Prophet joined in heartily...

'Grant Thy Mercy on us Lord,
All the Helpers and the Emigrants...'

'Ali and Zayd stopped what they were doing and stared at the Prophet. He hadn't rhymed the last verse.

'O Messenger', ventured Abu Bakr, 'Why did you change around the last words?'

'Did I?' said the Prophet innocently. 'Well now, the Makkans insist that the Quran is a fake and that I am a poet, but you can see for yourselves, I can't even make a proper rhyme!'

14
Madina II

After seven months, the mosque was completed. The brick and mud walls had been smoothed down and whitened; the tapering palm trunks were bent into graceful arches to support the rafters and palm branches of the roof. To the Believers, it was a beautiful sight. But one wealthy and powerful citizen of Madina thought otherwise.

'How long do you think this temple of yours will hold up?' he scoffed, looking up at the flimsy roof, and then at Muhammad. 'A house of prayer should be built of sturdy and durable materials!'

'Rafters and branches were sturdy enough for the Prophet Moses', answered Muhammad. 'Moreover, a thatched roof is more durable than man's fortune on this earth.'

Behind the mosque they had built the living quarters. It was there that the Prophet would soon bring his new wife, little 'Aisha, Abu Bakr's daughter. She was a lively and sometimes mischievous girl, and she kept the Prophet young at heart. Marriage with 'Aisha meant that the bond between the Prophet and his best friend would become even closer.

Muhammad was allowed by his religion to have more than one wife. Later, they too shared the apartments behind the mosque. Most of the wives he chose were widows; widows of the Believers who had died in battle, or of enemy chiefs, for whom marriage with Muhammad meant protection and security. In those days, life was hard for a widow, who was often neglected and taken advantage of. But none of these ladies ever replaced the Prophet's love for Khadija, who had been the first of the Believers, and the mother of his children.

Late one afternoon, when all the Helpers and Emigrants were gathered around the Prophet in the mosque, he asked them: 'How shall we call our people to prayer? The Christians have their gongs and their bells, the Jews have their trumpets and horns...'

The room fell silent. Had anyone a suggestion? Finally, an old man in the corner cleared his voice, 'If God's Messenger will permit', he said, 'I should like to tell of a dream...'

The Messenger nodded, and all leaned forward to hear.

'I had a vision one night of a man clad all in green. He held in his hand a bell. When I saw the bell, I thought to myself, "Why, that is what we need to call the Believers to prayer", so I offered to purchase it from him. But he refused, and told me: "I will show you a far better way... a human voice, a voice which can be heard from afar. A voice calling:

'GOD IS MOST GREAT! THERE IS NO GOD BUT GOD AND MUHAMMAD IS HIS PROPHET. COME TO PRAYER! COME TO PRAYER!'"

The Prophet closed his eyes a moment, then nodded. 'It is indeed a sign from God. A human voice, then, shall call the Believers to prayer.'

Abu Bakr had been sitting with his head bowed, listening and remembering. He had heard a voice once — never in all his life would he forget that voice.

He had been strolling on the outskirts of Makka, when it reached him from across the sands and heat of the desert. 'Ahad!' it cried, 'Ahad! One God, Only One!'

Such a cry of anguish and faith it was, that his heart melted upon hearing it, and he was compelled to go and see from whom it came. There, outside the city, he found Bilal, the slave. His huge ebony body was staked out and stretched across the sands. He was covered with red gashes from the whip, and an enormous boulder crushed down upon his chest. The sun had all but baked his bleeding lips; nevertheless, with a great effort he summoned up his strength and cried out his faith in defiance to the pain:

'Ahad! One God, Only One!'

Abu Bakr tugged at the boulder and rolled it away. Then he released the slave from his bonds and went to find Bilal's master.

'He is rebellious and stubborn', said the master with contempt. 'He refused to worship the gods of the Ka'ba.' Abu Bakr did not argue. He paid the ransom and that is how Bilal became a free man.

Seated beside the Prophet, Abu Bakr looked over the tall black man whose life he had saved, and who had shown such proof of faith. As he did so, the Prophet spoke.

'Bilal shall be the one to call the Prayer. Bilal shall be our Mua'dhdhin.'

'Yes! Bilal!' agreed the others.

It was Abu Bakr's turn to smile.

Bilal, slightly reluctant, and a bit embarrassed, let himself be hoisted to the top of a nearby building. There, facing again the vast sky and the open desert, he forgot his shyness. His beautiful voice rang out, resonant and compelling:

'ALLAAAAH HOO AKBAR! GOD IS MOST GREAT!
COME TO PRAYER! COME TO PRAYER!'

It called to the Believers below him, to the merchants in the marketplace who dropped what they were doing and looked up to listen. It was heard by the women in their homes and the children playing in the shade of the palm trees; the lonely traveller far out in the desert heard it too; and all of Madina knew, then, that this was the call to prayer of the new religion called Islam: Surrender to the One God.

Even now, after a thousand and four hundred years have passed, the call to prayer still rings out from every mosque in the world, five times a day.

That night, everyone gathered in the Prophet's new quarters to celebrate the completion of the building and the recent weddings: the Prophet's with 'Aisha and 'Ali's marriage with the Prophet's devoted daughter Fatima.

Abu Bakr had just started and said: 'In the name of God, the Merciful, the Compassionate,' when in rushed one of the Believers who had searched for work all day and was obviously starving. He flung himself down on a mat, and seeing that everyone else had already taken their share, grabbed a generous portion of mutton and began devouring it. Catching the Prophet's eye, he remembered that he had not said 'Bismillah', so he gulped down a mouthful and closed his eyes to pray. The Prophet threw back his head and laughed heartily.

'What is it, O Messenger?' asked the starving Believer. 'Would that you could have seen it!' laughed the Prophet. 'When you sat down and started to eat, the Devil was eating along with you, but when you stopped to say: In the name of God, the Devil threw up his portion and scampered off!'

84

15
The Battles: Badr

Although Muhammad was a Prophet of God, this did not prevent him from taking satisfaction in sweeping the floor of his quarters or in mending his own garments. This is just what he had been doing one morning while 'Aisha was stringing polished date seeds into a necklace for the cat.

'Aisha soon got bored with this and started dangling the string of date seeds up and down in front of the cat, who followed the movement lazily with huge green eyes, although he had no intention of leaving the Prophet's newly mended cloak upon which he had settled himself.

Time came for the Prophet to begin getting ready for the Friday prayers. He performed the ritual washing, as Gabriel had taught him, then carefully he combed his hair and beard, cleaned his teeth and applied a final touch of musk oil.

On entering the courtyard, the sight which met his eyes saddened his heart. Many of the Believers who had emigrated from Makka were thin and pale from want of food. To one side of the courtyard sat the 'People of the Bench' as he called them, because they had no homes and slept on benches in front of the Mosque at night. Others, like Abu Bakr, whose property and possessions had been taken over by the Quraysh, found no work for themselves in this city of farmers — they, who had been merchants.

Only yesterday, 'Ali had told the Prophet, he had spent the whole day carrying buckets of water for a man who was making bricks and had been paid only sixteen dates for his trouble. As it was, the Prophet himself often went hungry, or shared his meagre diet of dates and honey with those less fortunate.

The Prophet noticed on that Friday that many were not present. Some, like Fatima had contracted the fever which was so common amongst the Emigrants in the climate of Madina. Others had been charged by the Prophet to negotiate peace treaties with the tribes who had settled along the caravan routes to Makka. Absent, also, were the small patrols of men whom the Prophet sent out as a reminder to the Quraysh. For indeed the Quraysh needed reminding. They needed to be reminded that the Prophet and the Believers feared none but Almighty God, that they stood by their rights to profess their own religion, openly and freely; that they too had a right to make a yearly pilgrimage to Makka; and to call men to their new religion.

But soon, now, the time for these patrols would come to an end. On this Friday the Prophet had made a decision; that he would announce to his followers the new revelation which had been sent to him from Gabriel: the command to fight in the name of God against the unbelievers.

No one had slept peacefully that night in Madina. Above the city, huge black clouds had gathered and flashes of white lightening soundlessly streaked down the sky and pierced the earth.

The Prophet had spent the whole night in prayer, while 'Aisha tossed and turned fitfully on her mat.

Outside in the courtyard, Hamza's gaunt figure paced back and forth. His hunter's instinct was aroused and his eyes flashed this way and that as if in search of prey.

In his dark tent, Sa'd, the arrow maker, lay awake. Unconsciously, his hands clasped and unclasped themselves, as if handling the tools of his trade.

Abu Bakr, too, had spent a sleepless vigil crosslegged on his mat, repeating the most recent verses of revelation:

'Fight in the cause of God
Those who fight you...
And fight them on —
Until there is no more
Tumult or oppression
And there prevail
Justice and faith in God...'

Again and again he repeated these verses, wondering what future events they foretold.

Morning had come, but the storm clouds over Madina refused to break, and no rain fell to ease the tension in the air. Yet suddenly, everything and everyone was in motion, as if bestirred by an alarm. At the sound of Bilal's voice calling the Azan, the Believers rushed to the mosque. In moments the news spread and was on the lips of all those present:

A caravan of one thousand camels laden with untold wealth had left Damascus and was heading for Makka. The commander of this caravan was Abu Sufyan, the Chief of Makka. He who had posted the ban in the Ka'ba. He who had plotted the assassination of the Prophet of God.

A caravan of this size would not be left unprotected. Surely not! It would be accompanied by well-armed men!

In no time at all the commands issued by Muhammad were carried out. Helpers and Emigrants alike, with the Prophet and Abu Bakr in the lead prepared to set out from Madina by the upper route.

The Prophet passed his own banner on to Mu'sab, and 'Ali, grim faced, clasped Al Oqab, the eagle banner and raised it high above their heads. Hamza, at a sign from the Prophet marched forward with flashing eyes followed by 'Umar, Sa'd the arrow maker, and the faithful 'Ubayda. In all they numbered three hundred and fourteen men, with only seventy camels and two horses to carry them eighty miles out into the desert.

Yet on they walked and rode, under the burning sun, three or four at a time sharing one camel, the Prophet sharing his with Zayd and 'Ali.

But news travels faster than man. Abu Sufyan had sent to Makka for reinforcements and Abu Jahl was rounding up an army of one thousand men, armed and mounted! At this very moment they were setting out from Makka.

Hearing this, the Prophet reined in his camel and turned to his men. 'What do you advise now?' he asked.

'We will fight resolutely with you, no matter where', replied the Emigrants, and the Prophet blessed and thanked them. To the others he turned and asked 'Give me advice, O men!'

'If you mean us', answered the Helpers, 'we have given our word and agreement to hear and obey, go where you wish and we are with you. Even if you were to ask us to plunge into the sea, we would follow you — not a man would stay behind'.

The Prophet was delighted with these words, and greatly encouraged. 'Forward in good heart!' he exclaimed. 'For God has promised me a choice of two, and by God now it is as if I could see the enemy cut down!'

Meanwhile, Abu Sufyan's spies had discovered that the Believers were headed for the nearby wells of Badr. Hastily he ordered his caravan to divert their route and head full speed westward to the seashore, out of danger of Muhammad's men.

The commanders of the Quraysh army had already arrived a few miles south of Badr when the news reached them that Abu Sufyan's caravan was well away from Badr, and out of danger.

'Let us return to Makka, now that Abu Sufyan's caravan is safe', some advised. 'It is not right to spill the blood of a kinsman.'

'Never!' retorted Abu Jahl. 'By God we will not go back until we have been to Badr. We will spend three days there, slaughter camels and feast and drink wine... so come on!'

As night fell over Badr, one could hear, to the south, the loud voices of the Quraysh, with much boasting and drinking, and if one looked carefully, one could make out, a little to the northwest, the lights of the camp where Muhammad and his men lay waiting for the dawn attack.

'Abdullah, a not too young figure, sat beside the dying embers of the fire waiting for dawn. From out of the corner of his eye he could see a figure moving carefully towards the rear of the campsite. He made it out to be Mas'ud, a young man from Makka. Silently, 'Abdullah moved towards him and took him by the arm. Startled, the youth dropped his belongings and turned his face away. 'Abdullah led him to a side of the camp, where they could talk without disturbing the sleeping men.

Still avoiding 'Abdullah's eyes, the boy began to speak: 'I was going to leave the campsite', he said sullenly, 'I don't want to fight'. 'Abdullah waited for him to continue. 'When I made the declaration of faith, it was in full sincerity. I do believe that there is but One God and that Muhammad is indeed a Prophet of God. I understood this to mean we were to perform our regular prayers, to fast, to give alms, to help our brothers. There was no mention then of fighting. Why now, must we fight? Moreover, these are not strangers we are fighting, but our own neighbours — the Prophet's own family! Call me a coward if you like, I am no fighter, 'Abdullah.'

'You are lying, Mas'ud', replied 'Abdullah.

The youth looked up. 'What?', he said.

'You are lying, Mas'ud. You are a fighter. Do you think that battles take place only on the battlefield? I have known you since the day you stood before the Prophet and declared your faith — since before then, and I have seen you fight many battles. And you have won them. Every day you fight battles and win them. Every time you bow your head for the morning prayer and leave the comfort of your mat you have fought a battle, and won. Every time you give something away which you have need of yourself, you fight, and you win. All day long you fight battles against your own greed, your own comfort, and the attractions of the easy things of this world. When you study, rather than sit around and gossip about other people; when you share your food, as I have seen you do, and stay hungry; when you are accused of something and don't insist that you are in the right. When something is taken from you and you don't complain. Do not say you are not a fighter, Mas'ud.'

'Tomorrow', continued 'Abdullah, looking out onto the plains dimly lit by the moon, 'the Prophet will fight a battle against his own kinsmen... just as you fight battles against your own self. Because that part of you which will not listen to what is good and according to God's will, must be fought against and overcome. That is what we shall do tomorrow, Mas'ud. And with God's help, the battle here at the wells of Badr will stand out for all times as a sign... a symbol of man's fight against his lower self. That is the meaning of battles, in our religion of Islam, Mas'ud. I know this (he added softly)

90

because the Prophet himself has told me'.

Together they walked back to the campsite.

We're still young and life seems very long to us', continued 'Abdullah as they stood under the stars of Badr, 'but God's messenger said that compared to the Eternal life, our life here on earth will seem like a dream, when we have left it'.

'May God bless you, 'Abdullah', returned the other, after a pause. 'I'm going to rest a bit. We have one thousand Quraysh to deal with in the morning.'

At the break of dawn, the Prophet came out of the arbour of palm leaves erected for him close to the wells of Badr, and joined the other believers in the morning prayer.

As the sun rose over the desert, the Makkan army, led by Abu Jahl, streamed into the valley south of the wells. Muhammad looked down, and saw for the first time the strength and number of his enemies.

'Oh God!' prayed Muhammad, who had never in his life lifted his hand against another man, 'Oh God, here come the Quraysh in their vanity and pride, fighting against Thy cause and calling Thy prophet a liar... Oh God! If this handful of your worshippers are destroyed, there will be no one left to worship you'.

The two armies stood now, lined up, facing each other and preparing for single combat. Dressed in splendid armour and protected by guilded shields, the Quraysh commanders, goaded by Abu Jahl, shouted insults at the little band.

'By Hubal, we shall slay you all before the sun turns hot!' cried one.

'Show your courage, if you have any, or let us feed you to the flies', goaded another.

Three Quraysh generals strode forward out of the ranks brandishing scimitars and yelling, 'Let us see your faces that we may decorate them with your blood!'

In response, three young men from Madina leapt boldly forward to meet the challenge. 'Infidels' answered one. 'May you burn in the fires of Jahannam!'

'Who are these babies?' roared Abu Jahl scornfully. 'We have not come all this way to blunt our swords on sucklings from Madina... Makkan rebels, step forward!'

At a sign from the Prophet, 'Ali dashed out of the lines and along with him, Hamza, bold and fierce, an ostrich feather waving from his cuirass so that all would know who he was. Then followed 'Ubayda, Muhammad's cousin, old, but youthful in his courage.

Fiercely they fought and in seconds the three Quraysh commanders fell dead to the ground. But old 'Ubayda was carried off the battlefield mortally wounded.

'Shall I attain Paradise now?' he asked of the Prophet.

'Yes, indeed, 'Ubayda' answered Muhammad, leaning over him his eyes filled with tears. 'Indeed, you shall'.

Furiously Abu Jahl roared commands and three more Quraysh generals marched forward to replace the fallen. 'Ali lunged to the attack and made quick work of two. 'Join your comrades in Hell-fire', cried Hamza, thrusting his sword in a deathblow at the third.

Stunned, Abu Jahl heard Muhammad give the order for general combat. Warriors from both sides rushed into the mêlée. The morning wore on and the sun beat mercilessly down on the enemy. Driven desperate by thirst, the Quraysh soldiers attempted to approach the wells of Badr, guarded by Muhammad's archers; but at each attempt they were shot down. As the full body of the Quraysh army attacked, Muhammad seized a handful of dust and flung it in their direction. 'Confusion on their faces', he cried, and mounting a horse, he charged down the hill into the thick of the battle.

'Gabriel', he announced to his men, 'Gabriel with a thousand angels is falling upon the enemy!' At the same instant, a burning wind arose from behind him whipping up clouds of sand into the faces of the Quraysh. Blinded and stunned they staggered back: 'Allahoo Akbar — God is Most Great!' shouted the Believers victoriously. On rode the Prophet into the core of the fighting.

Before him, he spotted Abu Jahl, blindly swinging his scimitar right and left, wild with rage. In an instant, the Quraysh commander was thrown from his charger by the farm boys and to the very point of death, but did not cease cursing the Prophet.

'Abu Jahl is dead!' cried the Makkans in despair, and broke into flight, running for their lives from the advancing attack.

The Battle of Badr was over.

The Prophet retired to the hill, and prostrating his head on the sands, prayed: 'There is no god but God'!

As the sun descended to the west, the dead men were buried and prayers were held over them by the Prophet and the Believers. The booty was brought to the Prophet and distributed evenly according to the Laws of the Quran. Many prisoners were taken and Muhammad ordered that they be treated respectfully and given shelter in the tents of the Believers. The poor were invited to convert to Islam or were sent back to Makka, and the wealthy, too, were given the choice to convert, to remain as captives, or to be ransomed according to the wealth they possessed.

One by one the prisoners were brought before the Prophet to declare their choice.

'And what have we here?' cried Hamza, dragging forth a prisoner who was objecting furiously to the treatment.

'Is this not 'Abbas himself? Author of the "Lovesick Camel" and traitor to his own nephew?'

'Let me go, Hamza! What a way to treat a righteous man. There has been some horrible mistake!' he cried, turning towards the Prophet and struggling against Hamza's firm grip. 'What is all this nonsense... I only came to watch, not to fight! Surely you don't believe I would join in with that dreadful lot — I am a Believer! I shall remain faithful to my dear nephew till the very end', he pleaded, forcing tears to his eyes.

The Prophet shook his head and tried to refrain from smiling. 'Nonetheless, you were on the enemy's side. Let him pay his ransom and set him free', he ordered.

'Ransom!' exclaimed 'Abbas horrified. 'Surely you know that I am a poor and destitute man. Let us forget this talk of ransom. Set free your penniless uncle.'

'Even if it were true', replied Muhammad, 'we know you have deposited a goodly sum in your wife's name'.

'My wife? What wife?' cried 'Abbas, not daring to look the Prophet in the eye. But Hamza had had enough. 'Abbas was hurried away, and in the end declared his ransom as did the others.

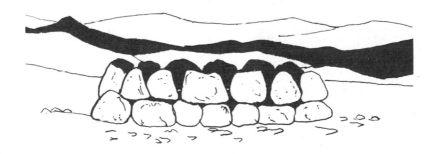

16
The Battles: Uhud

A year had passed since the battle of Badr. Abu Lahab, the Prophet's enemy had died in Makka shortly afterwards, of a fit of bad temper. With the exception of Khalid, the great cavalry leader, Abu Jahl and most of the prominent Makkan generals and chiefs had all been slain. The Quraysh of Makka, embittered by a year of mourning and thirsty for revenge, were eager for another battle. Abu Sufyan, as Makkan chief, had no difficulty raising an impressive sum in order to equip another army — three times more powerful than the last.

Three thousand soldiers, fully armed, a cavalry of two hundred horsemen under the command of Khalid, and last but not least, a band of bloodthirsty women, frantically beating timbrels and chanting the hymns of war, prepared to set out from Makka.

On the eve of departure, Khalid had a dream. In the dream, having passed in review his troops, examined horses and equipment and selected his own magnificent armour, he went to the Ka'ba to join the others in the sacrificial feasts.

As he prepared to leave the ceremony, the figure of a stranger standing under the rafters of the doorway, blocked his passage.

'If you wish to know the outcome of tomorrow's battle, then heed my words', he said.

Khalid, impressed by the stranger's manner and supposing him to be a soothsayer of the Ka'ba, made sign that he should continue.

'O Khalid, tomorrow's victory shall be in the hands of the Quraysh. The enemy will retreat and scatter before you like grains of sand. But in future times you will fight on the side of Muhammad, the Messenger of God. Your fame will shine all over Arabia, and beyond to Syria and Persia, and further still. You shall be known to all the world as the Sword of God.'

'Are you mad?' replied Khalid, 'I am fighting for our gods, against Muhammad and his religion, not for him. Islam is my enemy!'

'Let this be a sign to you' interrupted the stranger, 'Muhammad will be declared dead, and yet he shall live: You shall know, then, the truth of your fate, O Khalid Ibn El Walid,... Sword of God'.

Khalid, awed by the stranger, but horrified by his words, wished to press him further, but the figure had stepped through the doorway of the Ka'ba, and disappeared. And as he did so, Khalid awoke.

Muhammad was visiting the gardens of Quba and the very first mosque, for which he had lovingly laid the cornerstone after his long flight through the desert with Abu Bakr.

He led the prayers, and then addressed the Believers with verses from the Quran:

'When they advanced to meet Goliath and his forces,
They prayed: "O Lord! Pour out constancy on us
And make our steps firm:
Help us against those that reject faith!"
And by God's will they routed them,
And David slew Goliath...
...And had not God
Checked one set of people by means of another
The earth would indeed be full of mischief...'

After he had spoken, the Believers of Quba

gathered round, sharing their dates and fresh milk with him.

As he prepared to leave Quba, a courier arrived in great haste and handed him a letter. It was unsealed and read to the Prophet. It said:

'My dear Nephew,
You shall see now that your old uncle is no traitor after all. Pay close attention, for I do not write in jest. The Makkans, with an army of 3,000 men have set out to meet you in battle. Be you therefore forewarned.
And may victory be in your hands.

Your uncle: 'ABBAS'

Mounting Al-Qaswa, the Prophet rode back to Madina in a cloud of dust.

The following morning, a great debate arose between the elder and the young Believers. The Prophet, during the night had dreamt that his sword had been broken and his mount slaughtered. 'Would it not be better', he suggested, 'to remain in the city and defend it with arrows and stones from the rooftops?'. The elders agreed.

'If we remained in the city', reasoned Abu Bakr, 'the Quraysh would soon give up and beat a retreat'.

'Ali, Hamza and 'Umar were sure that after Badr, God would always be on their side: and that no army, not even an experienced army of 3,000 men against their 700, could stop them from winning.

'And besides,' added Hamza, 'if we remain barricaded within the city like a hoard of timid women, why we'll be the laughing stock of Arabia! Can't you see me now, with a handkerchief of date seeds, pelting the enemy from behind woven curtains?' The young men doubled up with laughter at his mimicry.

A while later the Prophet emerged from his

99

quarters dressed for battle. His chest and back were covered with a polished cuirass; a shield hung from his shoulder; a sword at his side. In his hand he held a bow, and on his head a spiked helmet bound by a black turban.

Hamza coughed and looked down. 'O Prophet of God,' he said humbly, 'perhaps we have been too hasty in our desire to fight the idol worshippers. Perhaps we had better reconsider...'

'It is not proper', replied Muhammad, 'for a Prophet of God to don his armour and then remove it'. So saying, he handed the white banner of Islam to Mus'ab, and mounting his horse, led his men out of the city.

Mount Uhud stood grim and bare over the arid plains below. The Prophet's men stood with their backs to the bleak mountain, facing the plains. The archers were told to position themselves on a mound towards the rear of the army. 'Keep guard over the rear position', commanded the Prophet, 'and do not move from that spot, whatever happens'.

The archers moved to the rear mound, some of them reluctantly.

'It's all very well for us to stay posted here until the end of the battle', grumbled one of them, 'if there is any booty, we shall be the last ones to get any'.

'Watch what you are saying' ventured his companion. 'Remember that our purpose is not for plunder, but to fight in the cause of God against the unbelievers.'

Meanwhile, from across the plain resounded the beating of timbrels and the battle songs of the Quraysh women. On marched the Makkan army, a tidal wave of colour and splendour. Perched high on a camel, the grotesque statue of Hubal lurched forward.

The first to step out from the Makkan ranks was the

100

Standard bearer of the Quraysh army. 'Ali's scimitar flashed in the sunlight, and a head rolled in the sand. Three more Makkans ran forward into battle. Striking the enemy with the full force of their faith and determination, they blasted through their ranks with the strength and courage of lions. Cries of 'Allahoo Akbar' rose above the chants of the women and the clashing of steel. They fought onward, and the Quraysh, overcome by their power, doubled under their blows, and fell back.

Khalid, mounted high on his steed, watched and waited. Now the Believers had fought their way into the Makkan camp; the Quraysh fell back further still, and cries of victory rang out amongst the Believers.

The archers, still posted high on the rear ground, caught a glimpse of the fabulous wealth of the Quraysh army.

'Why wait?' exclaimed some. 'The victory and the booty is ours!' Abandoning their posts, they dashed down to the Quraysh campsite to claim their due.

Khalid's keen eye had not missed their move. 'Charge!' he cried to his cavalry, and wheeling around they cantered past the abandoned spot and on behind the Prophet's lines. Right and left, the Believers fell under the hoofs and lances of Khalid's men. Panic seized them and they ran for their lives. The Quraysh, seeing the turn of events, charged forward with renewed strength. One of them cut Mus'ab to the ground. Mistaking him for the Prophet, the Makkan cried, 'I have killed Muhammad! Muhammad is dead!' Hearing this, many Believers abandoned all hope and began to retreat from the battlefield.

'Where are you going?' cried Muhammad, 'I am the Messenger of God... come back!' But they were too far away to hear.

Spotting the advantage, the Quraysh warriors

101

moved in for the attack. 'Ali and 'Umar rallied to the charge, but the Prophet fell to the ground, wounded on the mouth and head. 'Ali, Abu Bakr and 'Umar carried him to a hidden spot above the battle site.

The Quraysh, seeing that they had won, strode back to their camps. Abu Sufyan alone stayed behind. He looked around in vain. Where was Muhammad? Where was 'Ali and the others?

'Today is in exchange for Badr' he shouted to the void. 'Show thy strength, O Hubal!'

From behind a pile of rocks, 'Umar lashed back, 'Our dead are in Paradise, yours are in Hell fire!'

'Have we killed Muhammad?' cried Abu Sufyan.

'By God you have not!' was the response. 'He can hear you shouting!'

'We shall meet you next year at Badr', called back Abu Sufyan.

Slowly he headed back to the camp and joined Khalid.

'You and your magnificent cavalry have won us this victory' he said to him.

'They announced that Muhammad was dead, yet he was not' answered Khalid. 'Why didn't you slay him?'

Abu Sufyan said nothing for a long time. 'I don't know' he answered finally. 'But next year at Badr, your sword will finish him.'

Khalid was silent. He heard again, or had he imagined it... the voice of the stranger... 'Khalid Ibn El Walid, the Sword of God'.

On the arid plains of Uhud, Hamza the Hunter, and Mus'ab the standard bearer who had first instructed the Helpers in the religion of Islam, were buried.

'From God you came and to God you return', prayed the Prophet. 'Peace be upon you for that which you have endured, and may you be blessed in the Hereafter...'

Fatima, who had come from Madina to tend to her father's wounds and help bury the dead, gently led the Prophet away from the graves. Together with the remaining companions they left the battlefield.

As the tired warriors neared the gates of the city, they could hear the women weeping and mourning for the slain Believers of Madina.

'And Hamza', cried Muhammad, 'Alas for Hamza, who is there to wail for him?'

That night as the Prophet drifted off to sleep, he heard crying and lamentations by the mosque. Rising from his mat he saw by the dim light of the moon, the women of Madina mourning the death of Hamza.

The very next morning, the Prophet ordered the veterans of Uhud to arm themselves and to follow him in pursuit of the Quraysh. At nightfall, when they reached near the enemy campsite, he instructed his men to light 500 fires in view of the enemy.

'Hubal save us!' cried Abu Sufyan, seeing the hill ablaze with light, 'Muhammad has returned with a gigantic army!'

In no time at all, to the great satisfaction of the Prophet and his men, Abu Sufyan's victorious army had taken to its heels.

Back in Madina, the Prophet's voice rang out to the congregation of Believers:

'Did you think that you would enter Heaven
Without God testing
Those of you who fought hard in His cause
And remained Steadfast?
Muhammad is no more than a messenger:
Many were the messengers that passed away before him.
If he died or were slain,

103

Will you then turn back on your heels?...
...No soul can die
Except by God's leave.'

Later that night, in the courtyard of the mosque, 'Umar, still overcome by grief and rage, thought aloud: We were on the point of victory when you disobeyed the Prophet's command. You forgot that you were fighting in the cause of God against the idol worshippers. You gave in to the passion of greed for the bounty. Then, blinded by this passion you were deaf to the Prophet's plea to return and fight. No wonder that the angels, who would have helped you, turned back in disgust! Let this be a lesson: Whosoever places his desires above the command of God is himself no more than an idolater, and shall surely perish!

So reflecting, the fierce and faithful 'Umar walked off into the night.

17
The Battles: The Ditch

The months that followed were difficult ones for the Prophet and the Believers. Twice, those whose mission it was to spread the message of the One God, were ambushed. There were plots against the Prophet's life. There were secret alliances between tribes who opposed Islam and the Quraysh of Makka. But always there were new converts to the faith.

A year rolled by and the time came for the rendezvous at Badr. Abu Sufyan did not arrive for the appointment. The drought made it impossible for horses and camels to go on campaign. The Prophet, with his 1,500 men returned to Madina, but Abu Sufyan had not remained idle.

By the following year, Abu Sufyan had allied himself with other powerful tribes and had raised an army of 10,000 men. He had also made secret understanding with the Jews of Madina. The Prophet, who had only 3,000 soldiers and a small cavalry, announced that this time they would defend Madina.

Abu Sufyan's troops were already on the march when the Prophet called a meeting of his followers. Abu Bakr, 'Umar, 'Ali and Zayd joined him in the courtyard of the mosque while the younger men sat apart at a respectful distance.

At a sign from the Prophet, 'Umar explained their position. 'Along the north side, the city is protected by steep cliffs, along the east, the houses form a solid rampart. But the south and southeast side of the city, where the streets run into gardens and oasis, remains open to attack. The problem is, how do we defend the city from this point?'

Abu Bakr, 'Ali and Zayd discussed what measures could be taken, but after a while they fell silent. No one had come up with a solution.

'O Messenger of God' ventured a youth. 'Forgive my boldness, but it may be that I can solve your problem'.

The Prophet looked up and saw that the speaker was Salman, the Persian, who had become freed from slavery when he had adopted Islam.

'Speak then, Salman, and do not be shy for we have need of advice', answered the Prophet.

'I remember when I was young, in my country, there were often sieges on the city. By digging a large ditch along the exposed area, we prevented the enemy from entering. It would not be impossible to do the same at the south and southeast points of Madina'.

'What an extraordinary idea!' mumbled Abu Bakr, who had never heard of such a thing. 'We Arabs always fight face to face with our enemies, and have never resorted to such... ah... mm... trickery.'

'Trickery or not, it's an excellent idea!' said 'Umar.

'May God reward you, Salman, for your suggestion' concluded the Prophet. 'I hereby delegate you to be in charge of the Ditch.'

The work was begun immediately. Without hesitation, the Prophet stripped himself to the waist, and armed with a spade, was the first to dig in. Salman had organised the men in relays. Abu Bakr, 'Umar, 'Ali and Zayd all dug hard with the sun fiercely burning over their backs and carried earth in the laps of their clothes. Not a moment of daylight would be wasted. Spades and pickaxes clanged, while the Prophet's voice led them on in song:

'Emigrants and Helpers we,
For help O Lord we turn to Thee
Paradise our prize shall be...'

While the Believers responded in chorus:

'To God's Messenger have we
Pledged our faith and loyalty
To fight against his enemy
O Lord from death we'll never flee!'

Among the men of Madina there were those whom the Prophet called 'The Hypocrites'. Those who declared their belief in God and in the Prophet's mission but in secret amongst themselves would ridicule and criticise him.

'There goes one now' said 'Ali to Zayd.

'How do you know?' asked Zayd.

'He threw down his spade and left the site without permission' answered 'Ali.

Barely was the ditch finished when the Quraysh army appeared on the plains of Madina.

The Prophet's men quickly stationed themselves. The archers were positioned directly behind the ditch.

'Charge' bellowed Abu Sufyan. The Makkan cavalry charged — and came to a halt.

'Charge', repeated Abu Sufyan. Then he saw the ditch. Abu Sufyan was flabbergasted. 'What kind of warfare is this?' he screamed over the empty ditch. A volley of arrows answered his shout. 'We did not come here to play games, Muhammad!' Come out in the open field and fight!'

Another volley of arrows greeted this challenge. And so it continued, day after day, the Quraysh shouting insults and the Believers returning insults with arrows.

Meanwhile, the Prophet was concerned. It was

rumoured that one of the Jewish tribes of Madina — the very tribe guarding the rear of the city — were planning to accept bribes from the Quraysh. Muhammad, who was worried that his followers, especially the Helpers, might not be able to stand the onslaught any longer, came up with an idea, which he shared with his men. 'Do you think if we offer one of Abu Sufyan's tribes a third of our date crop they would go home?'

'Do you propose this as a command of God, or is it an idea of your own?' asked one devout follower.

The Prophet smiled. 'If it had been a command of God, I would not have asked your advice? I merely thought it would relieve our plight.'

'O Messenger of God', responded the other. 'When we were lowly idolaters, we never gave them our dates for nothing. Now that we are led by the true faith, shall we just hand over our crops? If they want dates, let them fight for them!' The Prophet's face beamed with approval.

Finally, one day, Abu Sufyan had had enough. 'I say we can cross that ditch, and by Hubal we will! You, 'Amir!' he called to a gigantic warrior on horseback. 'Take your swiftest and most nimble horse and make it fly like a bird to the other side.'

To the concern of the Believers, 'Amir's horse, after a few tries, did just that. In one leap it cleared the ditch and pranced victoriously in front of Muhammad's men. 'Ali, the Lion of God was not afraid. He was no match for this giant, but the Prophet's prayers redoubled his courage. Frantically, at first, he slashed the air, while 'Amir laughed in ridicule. With a thrust of his sword 'Ali defeated the giant.

While more and more Quraysh cavalrymen attempted the breach, day after day Muhammad's men fought to keep them off. Even though the women were lodged far off, they didn't hesitate to go right out amongst the fighting, dressing wounds and carrying water to the Believers.

Finally, the weather, as if in answer to the Prophet's prayers, grew bitterly colder. Abu Sufyan's soldiers were cut to the bone by the winter winds. Tents were blown away, and their horses starved for lack of fresh grass. An icy rain followed, drowning all their courage. Abu Sufyan, sick with a cold and exhausted gave up. Ordering the siege to be lifted he returned with his army to Makka.

Almost as soon as the Makkans had gone, the warm sun and gentle breezes returned to Madina.

The Prophet's men looked out upon the empty plains and raised a cry of gratefulness: 'Allahoo Akbar — God is Most Great!' They put down their swords and bows and shields and formed a line behind the Prophet who then began the morning prayer:

'Glory to Thee O God, and Thine is the praise, and Blessed is Thy name and exalted Thy Majesty and there is none to be served beside Thee...'

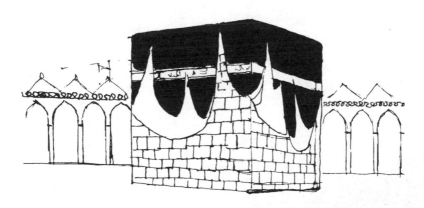

18
The Return

One night the Prophet dreamed he had returned to Makka, peacefully and on pilgrimage. There had been no fighting, no opposition.

In fact, the Prophet had been yearning since he had arrived in Madina to make the pilgrimage to the Holy City of Makka and to pray once again at the Sacred Ka'ba. The Emigrants, too, homesick after six years of exile — six years of poverty and battles, were eager to join him. The Prophet knew his dream was a divine promise.

So they set out, one morning during the appropriate month. One thousand five hundred pilgrims on camels, the Prophet in the lead. Al-Qaswa, freshly groomed, white and proud, padded peacefully in the direction of the Holy City.

But the Quraysh in Makka, who had got word of their arrival could not bear the idea of the man they considered their arch enemy returning back triumphantly and performing pilgrimage. They would not allow this at any cost, they decided.

When the pilgrims arrived at Hudaybiya, eight miles from Makka, a messenger arrived from the Quraysh to inquire as to their intentions. The Prophet replied that their intentions were peaceful and that they wished only to enjoy their natural right and perform the pilgrimage. Then, just to assure them, the Prophet sent 'Uthman as a go-between.

But 'Uthman did not return when expected, and the Believers became anxious. Had he been killed?

Would the Quraysh raise up an army against them? How would they defend themselves, since they were unarmed?

The Prophet, then, sensing that despite being unprepared he might have to fight, asked the Believers to renew their oath of loyalty. The same oath which the Helpers had taken one night seven years ago, in the valley of 'Aqaba.

Standing under a lonely acacia tree in the rocky plains of Hudaybiya, the Prophet slapped hands with each man who stepped forward to pledge his faith.

Time passed, and still no news came from Makka. Anxiously they scanned the horizon till finally a camel was seen in the distance. The messenger from Makka had arrived. The Makkans were in no mood to allow a peaceful pilgrimage. Instead they insisted, just to satisfy their pride, that Muhammad must go back that year without pilgrimage, and come back the next to fulfil their desire. They also wanted a truce. After a discussion, the peace terms were written down by 'Ali, and read to the Believers:

To Muhammad and his followers:
1. There will be no war between the parties for two years and they will live in peace.
2. Muslims should return this year and return for pilgrimage of the Ka'ba next year, keeping their swords sheathed, and stay for just three days in Makka.
3. The Arab tribes will be free to conclude alliances with any of the contracting parties.
4. Trade caravans of the Quraysh passing through Madina will not be interfered with.
5. If any one of the Quraysh goes to Madina without the consent of the party, he should be returned. But a Muslim coming to Makka from Madina will not be returned.

Astonished and disappointed, the Believers watched as the Prophet signed the truce. 'Umar was beside himself and went ranting to Abu Bakr.

'What! Is not Muhammad the Prophet of God? Are we not Believers? Are they not Infidels? Then why are we allowing this insult? It is the right of every Arab to make pilgrimage to the Ka'ba, every year! On top of it all, are we supposed to return those who come to us accepting Islam and not claim those who go to Makka? Why shall we accept those humiliating terms?'

Abu Bakr answered quietly but forcefully. 'God's Messenger does not like war for the sake of war. As Prophet of God he sees and knows the results of actions which neither you, 'Umar, nor I, can possibly foretell. You had best be patient and await the outcome of this truce.'

Shortly afterwards, the battle against the treacherous tribes of Khaybar was fought. And the Prophet's new banner, 'Uqab, the Black Eagle, waved victoriously over the oasis.

Once the truce was signed, many of the local tribes realised that the balance of power had shifted to the side of Islam and therefore they began to come to swear allegiance to the new religion.

Embassies were sent out to nearby kingdoms bearing letters sealed with the silver seal of the Prophet. To the court of Heraclius who became aware of the truth but did not have the courage to accept Islam; to the Negus of Abyssinia who had befriended many of the Believers during the time of the Ban, and who responded by sending his respects and embracing Islam. To the Roman Governor of Egypt who sent many presents to the Prophet, and finally to the Emperor of Persia himself, who tore up the epistle.

'Just as he tore the letter, so God will rend his empire', declared the Prophet casually.

113

In later years the prophesy came true, and all of Persia was united under the Prophet's banner.

A year had passed.

Khalid Ibn El Walid stood alone in the darkness outside his tent and looked down over Makka. He had camped some distance from Abu Sufyan and the others because he preferred to be alone. He was a warrior at heart and had little in common with the merchants of the city. Besides, he had heard and seen things that day which he needed time to understand. To do so he needed to feel the rugged terrain of the hills beneath his feet and the expanse of the night around him.

Early that morning, Abu Sufyan, in accordance with the treaty signed by the Prophet the year before, led the Makkan inhabitants out of the city to the hills, so that the Prophet and his followers might make the Holy pilgrimage into the city.

Shortly after dawn they arrived. Two thousand pilgrims, dressed in clean white unseamed garments poured into the valley like a vast white cloud, their Prophet in the lead.

From the top of the hill, Khalid watched this man who could act like a warrior and called himself a Prophet, lead his procession through the empty streets of the city. He heard their cries, like a chorus of victory: 'Labaik, Labaik! We are here, O Lord, we have come!' The procession then grew silent. Muhammad stepped up to the black stone of the Ka'ba and touched it reverently with his staff. Then, seven times he circled the Ka'ba and behind him followed the pilgrims like some huge battalion of angels, chanting: 'There is no god but God! He hath upheld His servant and exalted His people. He has put to flight the idolaters'.

Then Khalid watched the Prophet lead the procession from Safa to Marwa seven times, as Hagar had done in olden times when she went searching for

114

water for Isma'il.

Then followed more rituals; the shaving of heads and the sacrificing of camels.

That night the pilgrims camped in Makka, while the Prophet retired alone to the inner chamber of the Ka'ba.

Then, in the silence before dawn, Bilal climbed to the roof of the Ka'ba to announce the morning prayer. The first Islamic call to prayer ever to be heard in Makka.

The chant resounded over the silent city and echoed to the north, south, east and west. The sound of 'Allahoo Akbar — God is Most Great' rose even to the hills above. There, Khalid heard it, and was touched. As he watched, the two thousand pilgrims, led by the Prophet, began the prayer. Their forms in the white sunlight bowed and rose regularly, rhythmically. Khalid saw, and was transfixed. He began to understand then, what it was, this religion of the One God.

On the third day, the pilgrims left the empty city and returned to Madina.

Not long afterwards, Khalid, in full battle array, rode into the courtyard of the mosque at Madina, and declared to the Prophet and all who came to watch, his belief in the One God and in His Messenger.

Finally, two years after the truce, an event came about which broke the agreement of peace between the Quraysh and the Believers. A tribe which had sworn allegiance to the Quraysh attacked a tribe which had sworn allegiance to the Believers, and killed them even while they took refuge in the Sacred Mosque, where no blood is to be shed. The Makkans helped their allies.

However, they soon realised their mistake and trembled at the fact. What could be done? Their own people had broken the truce of Peace. The Prophet's army, stronger now by thousands, was sure to descend upon them. Abu Sufyan's army, greatly reduced because so many tribes had abandoned it, had lost its arrogance and Abu Sufyan himself had been humbled. Hesitatingly, one day he went alone to Madina to see what could be done. The Prophet and his men ignored him, and he returned to Makka more frightened than before.

The very same day the Prophet prepared to march on Makka. While 'Uqab, the Black Eagle, watched from his unfurled banner, the Prophet in his quarters prayed that their march to Makka might remain a secret. Firm instructions were issued and the commanders took up the word and announced it to their men.

'All roads to Makka shall be barred. All nomads shall be cautioned and stopped. Anyone who writes a letter to a Makkan shall wish his hand had never written it. Not a soul shall breathe a word of this nor shall trumpets sound nor cheering be heard on the way.'

On marched ten thousand men under the command of the Prophet himself through little-known terrain and along untrodden and stony paths. Not a word of their coming had been heard. The Prophet's secret had been kept. His orders had been followed.

When they had travelled half way to Makka, 'Umar spotted something not far ahead. 'By God!' he bellowed. 'Who is that I see coming from Makka? I swear, O Messenger of God, that none of our people have revealed the secret'.

The Prophet, to 'Umar's surprise, was not concerned. He merely shook his head and smiled.

The traveller approached. 'Good morning, good morning and may peace be upon you, nephew!' cried the familiar voice of 'Abbas. 'Out for a little stroll, I see' he added, completely ignoring the army of ten thousand men behind the Prophet. 'If you don't mind, my family and I would like to join you!'

'Do you and your family declare there is but One God and that Muhammad is a Prophet of God?' interrupted 'Umar suspiciously.

'That goes without saying', shrugged 'Abbas. 'Whatever you like, but don't wave that lance at my belly'.

'Uncle', responded the Prophet. 'You are the last of the Emigrants, as I am the last of the Prophets.'

The huge army marched on, silently, steadily towards Makka.

Within sight of Makka, the Prophet's army camped for the night. To the west and to the east blazed the lights of more than a thousand camp fires.

Abu Sufyan, from his post in Makka, gazed up at the lights from the fires and his heart sank. He had been tricked once in this way, but this time he had a foreboding suspicion that there were as many men as there were fires. Cautiously he set out from Makka to discover what fate had in store for the people of Makka.

The night was dark, but the fires lit the way as Abu Sufyan carefully climbed up to the Prophet's camp. Suddenly, what appeared to be a ghostly shape loomed menacingly up before him. 'Al-Lat protect me!' he bleated as the ghost turned into the form of a white mule.

'Hah!' cried a voice. 'It's a good thing I found you, Abu Sufyan, and it's a good thing you came this way', said 'Abbas from atop the Prophet's white mule. 'Up yonder you see the fires of an army of ten thousand men. You'd better cast your lot in with us, for there's no way you can defeat them. Come along to my nephew's tent before it's too late. Now climb up behind me and keep still.'

'What a humiliation!' thought Abu Sufyan dismally. 'To ride on the back of a mule behind this jokester, and

117

what's more to be led to Muhammad's tent like a goat to slaughter.'

'Halt!' cried 'Umar springing out of the darkness. 'Who goes there? Come, my sword, and place a kiss of welcome on this rascal's neck!' he cried, upon recognising Abu Sufyan.

'Put that thing away', chided 'Abbas, 'and allow this fellow a chance to meet with my nephew'. Upon which 'Umar reluctantly withdrew.

The next morning, Abu Sufyan was brought to the Prophet's tent. He avoided the Prophet's eyes while the latter looked long and hard at him. 'Abu Sufyan', said the Messenger of God in a soft voice, 'Abu Sufyan, have you not yet discovered that there is but One God?'

Abu Sufyan's mouth twisted into a scowl.

'Abbas shook him and hissed, 'This is no time for games, Sufyan, say it and be done with!'

'Umar's voice rang out darkly from a corner of the tent: 'Perhaps I could persuade you...'

Abu Sufyan reluctantly mumbled the words into the folds of his garment, and was told to rise.

'Now then', said the Prophet. 'Hasten to Makka. Let it be known that no one who takes refuge in the house of Abu Sufyan shall be harmed this day!'

Abu Sufyan hurried away to deliver the message to his people, but he did not miss seeing the forces of Arab clansmen, each with their own banner preparing to march, nor the chivalry of Madina in black mail and carrying shining lances.

'O Quraysh!' shouted Abu Sufyan as he arrived, 'Muhammad is close upon us! He has an army which cannot be withstood! Flee to your homes, or to my house, or to the Ka'ba, and you shall be safe!'

Hiding behind their doors and peering out through the windows, the Makkans watched and waited. What they saw finally drew cries of awe from them all. From

118

the south came Khalid's great cavalry of bedouin tribes. From the north came the battalions under Azd, from the west the Helpers of Madina under Sa'd, from the east the Emigrants led by 'Ubayda, and behind them all rode Muhammad, flanked on each side by Abu Bakr, 'Umar, and 'Ali commanding the black-armoured lancers.

Except for a short skirmish in the southern quarter, the columns of the Prophet's army entered the city peacefully.

From his post, just above Makka, the Prophet gave thanks to Almighty God Who had given him victory over the idolaters. Under the proud banner of Al 'Uqab, he watched as the four divisions of his army proceeded to occupy the city from their various points. Below him he could see the streets of Makka, the home of Abu Talib where he had been raised as a child, the house of Khadija, which had been his own, Abu Bakr's quarters, from where he began his flight to Madina, and the Holy Ka'ba, where on starry nights, wrapped in his grandfather's great cloak, he had listened to the tales of the Well of Zam-Zam, and the One Hundred Camels.

Behind him, on higher ground, the Prophet could see the cemetery of Makka, where lay the grave of Khadija, like a silent witness to the events below.

Muhammad changed into pilgrim's dress and descended from his post to the Ka'ba. There, before the eyes of the Makkans and his army of 10,000 men, he touched again the sacred stone and circled the Ka'ba seven times.

Then, standing before the great ugly statue of Hubal, he repeated these words:

'Truth is come and falsehood is vanished. Truly, falsehood is vanished'.

The gigantic statue tottered on its pedestal and crashed to the ground in pieces.

119

Muhammad, then took the key to the Ka'ba and ordered that all the idols within be demolished.

A crier was sent throughout the city proclaiming, 'Whosoever believes in God and in the Day of Judgement, let him not leave any image unbroken'. From out of windows and doorways, idols of all sorts and shapes were thrown into the street, and the people, seeing that no harm had come of it, breathed a sigh of relief.

Muhammad, the last Prophet of God, died two years later. Before his death, he was to make a last pilgrimage, at the end of which, he delivered a sermon:

'And so, I have fulfilled my mission. I have left amongst you a book, a plain command, the book of God. If you hold to the advice therein, you will never go astray.

'O Lord, I have delivered my message and accomplished my work!

'O Lord, I beseech Thee, bear Thou witness to it'.